James Hadley Chase and The Murder Room

》》》 This title is part of The Murder Room, our series dedicated to making available out-of-print or hard-to-find titles by classic crime writers.

Crime fiction has always held up a mirror to society. The Victorians were fascinated by sensational murder and the emerging science of detection; now we are obsessed with the forensic detail of violent death. And no other genre has so captivated and enthralled readers.

Vast troves of classic crime writing have for a long time been unavailable to all but the most dedicated frequenters of second-hand bookshops. The advent of digital publishing means that we are now able to bring you the backlists of a huge range of titles by classic and contemporary crime writers, some of which have been out of print for decades.

From the genteel amateur private eyes of the Golden Age and the femmes fatales of pulp fiction, to the morally ambiguous hard-boiled detectives of mid twentieth-century America and their descendants who walk our twenty-first century streets, The Murder Room has it all. 》》》

The Murder Room
Where Criminal Minds Meet

themurderroom.com

T0352158

James Hadley Chase (1906–1985)

Born René Brabazon Raymond in London, the son of a British colonel in the Indian Army, James Hadley Chase was educated at King's School in Rochester, Kent, and left home at the age of 18. He initially worked in book sales until, inspired by the rise of gangster culture during the Depression and by reading James M. Cain's *The Postman Always Rings Twice*, he wrote his first novel, *No Orchids for Miss Blandish*. Despite the American setting of many of his novels, Chase (like Peter Cheyney, another hugely successful British noir writer) never lived there, writing with the aid of maps and a slang dictionary. He had phenomenal success with the novel, which continued unabated throughout his entire career, spanning 45 years and nearly 90 novels. His work was published in dozens of languages and over thirty titles were adapted for film. He served in the RAF during World War II, where he also edited the RAF Journal. In 1956 he moved to France with his wife and son; they later moved to Switzerland, where Chase lived until his death in 1985.

By *James Hadley Chase*
(published in The Murder Room)

No Orchids for Miss
  Blandish
Eve
More Deadly Than the Male
Mission to Venice
Mission to Siena
Not Safe to Be Free
Shock Treatment
Come Easy – Go Easy
What's Better Than Money?
Just Another Sucker
I Would Rather Stay Poor
A Coffin from Hong Kong
Tell it to the Birds
One Bright Summer
  Morning
The Soft Centre
You Have Yourself a Deal
Have This One on Me
Well Now, My Pretty
Believed Violent
An Ear to the Ground
The Whiff of Money
The Vulture Is a Patient Bird
Like a Hole in the Head

An Ace Up My Sleeve
Want to Stay Alive?
Just a Matter of Time
You're Dead Without Money
Have a Change of Scene
Knock, Knock! Who's There?
Goldfish Have No Hiding
  Place
So What Happens to Me?
The Joker in the Pack
Believe This, You'll Believe
  Anything
Do Me a Favour, Drop Dead
I Hold the Four Aces
My Laugh Comes Last
Consider Yourself Dead
You Must Be Kidding
A Can of Worms
Try This One for Size
You Can Say That Again
Hand Me a Fig Leaf
Have a Nice Night
We'll Share a Double Funeral
Not My Thing
Hit Them Where It Hurts

Not My Thing

James Hadley Chase

An Orion book

Copyright © Hervey Raymond 1983

The right of James Hadley Chase to be identified as the author of this
work has been asserted in accordance with the Copyright, Designs and
Patents Act 1988.

This edition published by
The Orion Publishing Group Ltd
Orion House
5 Upper St Martin's Lane
London WC2H 9EA

An Hachette UK company
A CIP catalogue record for this book is available from the British Library

ISBN 978 1 4719 0414 1

All characters and events in this publication are fictitious and any
resemblance to real people, living or dead, is purely coincidental.

No part of this publication may be reproduced, stored in a retrieval system
or transmitted in any form or by any means without the prior permission
in writing of the publisher, nor be otherwise circulated in any form of
binding or cover other than that in which it is published without a similar
condition, including this condition, being imposed on the subsequent
purchaser.

www.orionbooks.co.uk

1

A tall, handsome man, in his late thirties, with dark curly hair, paused in the doorway leading to the élite gambling room of the Paradise City's casino. Immaculately dressed in an off-white suit, a dark-blue shirt and a blood-red tie, he surveyed the scene.

The time was 22.30. This room, containing only three roulette tables, was reserved for the high rollers. The lowest stake came at $500, and the tourists and the little gamblers kept well away. The ornate room was crowded for Paradise City, Florida, was the billionaires' playground.

Known in the underworld as Julian 'Lucky' Lucan, the tall man nodded his approval. Somewhere in this crowded room there would be a woman who would satisfy his greed for money.

Lucan's speciality was middle-aged women or elderly widows who had more money than sense. He led a life of luxury. If he had to bed with some fat old woman, he bedded her, giving her a late-life thrill, but he always saw the price was right, and it always came high.

He had been in Paradise City for the past three days. No matter how much money he received for his services, he was continually short. This didn't worry him. Lucan lived well and played the horses. Money was made to be spent. So far, he had been successful in finding a generous old woman, but these past three days hadn't produced anyone rich enough to be worthy of his charm. Lucan was an optimist. It was a matter of patience and circulating, but he was aware that his capital was dwindling. Why had he put $5000 on a nag that had come in last?

His bright blue eyes scanned the women seated at the tables. Maybe that fat one with the blue rinse and

1

smothered with diamonds might be interesting. Or there was that skinny old woman who must have had at least five face-lifts, wearing interesting rubies and emeralds. Both these women looked bored and lonely as they pushed $1000 plaques onto the table. The time to pounce was when they won, and then they would be in a receptive mood. He moved further into the room, took out a gold cigarette-case, given him by a French countess, selected a cigarette and lit it with a gold, diamond-encrusted lighter, given him by an aging Roumanian millionairess.

'Mr Lucan, I think?'

Lucan stiffened. A man's voice: curt and hard. He turned swiftly to find himself confronted by a powerfully built man of his own height, around fifty years of age, with black, close-cut hair, streaked with grey, blunt features and cold grey eyes.

Because of his profession, Lucan had made a study of men and women, and he immediately recognized that this man came into the category of 'Big People'. Apart from the cold, ruthless face, the man's dark suit must have cost heavy money. To his irritation, Lucan had to admit that this man's clothes, his finely woven white shirt and sombre hand-painted tie made him feel slightly shabby.

He put on his arrogant expression, trying to match this man's penetrating stare, but was forced to shift his gaze.

'I'm Lucan,' he said. 'I don't think we've met.'

'Mr Lucan, I may have a lucrative proposition for your consideration,' the man said. His voice low and harsh. 'Will you have a drink with me?'

A lucrative proposition.

Lucan became alert. He could smell money oozing out of this man, but he remained cautious.

'That's interesting.' He switched on his charming smile that had seduced so many elderly women, but it seemed to bounce off this man. 'And you? Who are you?'

2

'Shall we go to the bar, Mr Lucan? We can talk quietly,' and, turning, the man led the way from the roulette room, down a short passage to the almost deserted bar room.

Lucan followed him like a well trained dog.

A lucrative proposition.

Well, at least, he could listen. This man, he was sure, wasn't a time-waster.

The man selected a table in a dimly lit corner, away from the few drinkers who were consoling themselves for their losses. As Lucan sat down, the barman arrived.

'You drink . . . what?'

'A Scotch, thank you.'

'Two Scotches, Charles. Doubles.'

The man stared across the room, saying nothing. Lucan moved uneasily. He crushed out his cigarette.

'You didn't tell me your name.'

The man ignored him as he continued to stare into space. Glancing at him, Lucan felt his unease increase. Jesus! he thought, he's a real toughie. He had a face that could have been carved out of granite. Lucan shifted in his chair, and was relieved when the barman came with the drinks.

As soon as the barman had gone, the man turned and stared at Lucan. His steel-grey eyes probing and unpleasantly searching.

'I know all about you, Lucan,' the man said in his low hard voice. 'You are a successful vulture who preys on stupid, rich old women. You have no scruples. You will do anything if the money is big enough.'

Lucan stiffened, flushing.

'I don't know who the hell you are,' he blustered, 'but I'm not accepting insults from anyone!'

'Don't give me that crap!' the man snapped. 'I need a man like you, and the pay-off is big. I'm talking of two hundred thousand dollars.'

Lucan sucked in his breath. For two hundred thousand dollars he was prepared to accept any insult. He relaxed back in his chair.

'That sounds interesting,' he said.

The man regarded him, his steel-grey eyes showing contempt.

'I want to hire you to get rid of my wife.'

Lucan became completely relaxed. In the past, he had fixed more than a dozen divorces, and the pay-off had been peanuts in comparison to this man's proposal.

'No problem,' he said. 'You want a divorce . . . I'll fix it.'

'Pay attention!' The snap in the man's voice made Lucan stiffen again. 'I didn't say anything about a divorce. I said I wanted to hire you to get rid of my wife.'

Lucan stared at the hard, ruthless face and felt a qualm.

'I don't think I understand,' he said slowly.

'I want you to arrange that my wife has a lethal accident for which I will pay you two hundred thousand dollars in cash,' the man said.

A lethal accident!

Was this man a nut? Lucan wondered. He was telling him he wanted his wife murdered!

His voice unsteady, he said, 'I don't think I'm with you. I don't understand what you are saying.'

The man glared at him.

'I can't put it plainer. I want you to arrange that my wife has a lethal accident for which I will pay you two hundred thousand dollars.'

Lucan gulped.

'You – you are proposing that I murder your wife for two hundred thousand dollars?'

This was incredible!

'It seems at last, Lucan, you understand what I am proposing,' the man said.

4

Lucan's first reaction was to jump to his feet and leave the bar, but the inbred greed in him restrained him.

Two hundred thousand dollars!

Don't rush this, he told himself. Hear what this man has to say. There's always time to duck out.

'Well, I wasn't expecting this,' he said, taking out his handkerchief and touching his sweating temple. Then he drank all the Scotch in his glass. 'Are you serious?'

'Don't fart about!' the man snapped, moving impatiently. 'This is a proposition. Is it yes or no?'

Lucan's quick, cunning mind moved into action. This would be murder and he had no intention of having anything to do with that kind of thing. Stupid, rich old women, yes, but murder, no! All the same the pay-off couldn't be dismissed. Such a sum would clear his gambling debts and allow him to remain in this city of luxury for the season and forget the dreary old women.

'Yes or no?' the man repeated.

Lucan hesitated, then said cautiously, 'I think I might be able to help you.'

For the first time since they had met, the man gave a wry, grim smile.

'It's remarkable,' he said, half aloud, 'what money can buy.'

Lucan scarcely heard him. His mind now was in top gear. Among his numerous underworld associates, he knew several who wouldn't hesitate to waste anyone so long as the price was right. He would act as go-between, take his share of the loot and then forget the whole business.

Now, relaxed, he looked at the man who was staring watchfully at him.

'You must understand that this kind of thing isn't my scene,' he said, 'but I have connections. It can be arranged. Would you give me a couple of days to look around?'

'And *you* must understand,' the man said, menace in his

voice, 'this has to be utterly foolproof. A convincing lethal accident, and no come-back. Yes, have a couple of days. I expect a watertight, foolproof plan. Where are you staying?'

'At the Star Motel.'

'Then the day after tomorrow, we will meet there at eleven in the morning. I expect you to have arranged this to my satisfaction.' The man stood up. 'Good-night to you,' and he walked swiftly out of the bar and out of sight.

Lucan gave him three minutes, then, leaving the bar, he went to the entrance of the Casino.

The doorman touched his cap.

'Can I call your car, sir?'

Lucan extracted a ten-dollar bill from his wallet.

'No, thanks.' He folded the bill. 'Who was that tall gentleman who has just left? I seem to recognize him.'

'Why, that's Mr Sherman Jamison,' the doorman said, eyeing the bill.

'I thought it must be.'

The bill exchanged hands, then Lucan hurried to the car park, got in his rented Mercedes L 200 and drove onto the boulevard.

In the Casino's VIP car park, Sherman Jamison sat in his Silver Ghost Rolls Royce, his mind active.

'I have started the operation,' he thought. 'It now remains to see if this man can fix the problem.'

He admitted to himself that he was uneasy about dealing with Lucan: a greedy, slimy gigolo, but he had no alternative. He had no connections with likely killers who could be hired, although he was sure there must be many of them. He had to depend on Lucan who would be reasonably safe as a go-between, and seemed confident he could find the right man. What he had been told by a frustrated, elderly rich woman that 'That scoundrel will do anything for money' seemed to be proving correct.

6

Jamison warned himself that he would have to be very careful when dealing with Lucan. At least, he had a month's leeway. The plan had to be perfect: no police: a straight forward, unfortunate lethal accident. Nothing crude. In two day's time, he would know if Lucan could come up with the right plan, then, of course, he would have to be doubly careful.

His mind then switched to his wife, Shannon. They had been married for eight years. On the credit side, she was fair and handsome, an excellent hostess, which was important to his business connections. She organized his two homes with smooth efficiency, handling their staff firmly, but with kindness. She was loving and warm-natured. On the pillow, she was satisfactory, always willing when he wanted her. The debit side, however, weighed heavily against her.

Jamison's obsessional desire was to have a son. He had married Shannon when he was just over forty years of age. He had inherited the Jamison Computer Corporation from his father and had greatly increased its growth and potentials. He longed to have a son to inherit this great kingdom he and his father had built up. 'Always keep the company in the family,' his father had often said. Jamison wanted a son to guide him, teach him, to make him as successful as himself. When Jamison wanted something as badly as this, he made sure, no matter the means, of having it.

During the past six years, Shannon had had three miscarriages. None of these miscarriages were due to her own fault. She had exercised the utmost care, but they happened. As each miscarriage happened, Jamison became more and more hostile. Then last year, it looked as if they had succeeded. In her seventh month of pregnancy, Shannon tripped and fell down a flight of stairs. She was rushed to hospital. The baby was born dead . . . a son.

Jamison, looking at the tiny dead baby, felt a surge of frustrated, furious disappointment. He could scarcely bear to look at his wife. For two weeks, he kept away from her, travelling to London and Paris on business. Shannon had consulted the best specialists who assured her that this was a freak of nature, and there was no reason why she couldn't produce a son. In fact, they were certain of it. With their benign smiles, they told her to be patient and to try again. She got them to write to Jamison who was not impressed.

That was the first dangerous black mark against Shannon.

The second black mark, nothing like so serious, but still a black mark, was that Shannon was a strict Roman Catholic. Jamison was an agnostic and, when they married, Jamison accepted the fact that she had been brought up as an RC and had shrugged his shoulders, but when he realized that it would mean that Shannon attended Mass every morning, he grew bored and impatient with her religion, not having her with him at the breakfast-table.

Another thing he discovered about her was that she had considerable musical talent, playing the cello, and she insisted she attend the various musical festivals and NYC's many concerts. Any kind of music bored Jamison, so Shannon would go on her own to the various concert halls, leaving him to the continual round of cocktail parties and talking to visiting tycoons, taking them to nightclubs. The rift in their marriage rapidly expanded.

Then one evening while Jamison was attending a semi-business cocktail party and Shannon was in some concert hall, absorbed in listening to a Bach trio, he met Tarnia Lawrence.

He was talking to the President of an important bank, rather bored with the elderly man's waffling, when, looking beyond the President, he saw a tall, dark woman who had just come in. As she stood in the doorway before the host hurried to her side, Jamison regarded her with growing interest.

Jesus! he thought. Some woman!

Immaculately dressed in a simple evening gown that must have cost a lot of money, she was the most beautiful woman he had ever seen, and her figure set his blood moving.

The President was saying, 'The economic climate seems to be growing steadily worse . . .'

'Yes.' There was a snap in Jamison's voice. 'Do you know who that woman is?'

Startled, the President turned.

'Oh, of course. That's Miss Tarnia Lawrence. She is a client of ours.'

'Is that right?' Jamison continued to stare at the woman as the host led her across the room to a group of people. 'Who is she? What does she do?'

'Miss Lawrence is one of the most successful dress-designers in the business. She's doing amazingly well. I keep advising her to go public, but so far, she is hesitating. If she does, Jamison, I would advise you to take up a parcel of shares.'

'As good as that?' Jamison said, his eyes on the long, slim back and perfect hair-do.

'As good as that.' The President beamed. 'She owns three successful boutiques and a small factory. Her prices . . .' He rolled his eyes. 'My wife is nearly ruining me.'

'I would like to meet her,' Jamison said, feeling his pulse quicken.

'No problem,' the President said.

However, there was a problem as the woman was talking to a fat, pink-haired queer and, while the President and Jamison waited, the animated soft-spoken conversation seemed to Jamison to go on forever.

'Miss Lawrence only comes to these cocktails to do business,' the President whispered. 'It would be a bad time to interrupt her. This ghastly man is one of the important design cutters.'

'I can wait,' Jamison said, regarding this woman.

He thought she would be no more than thirty years of age. He studied her slim figure and her breasts. Again he felt a quickening of his blood. Yes! This was a woman!

The President began waffling again about the coming recession, but Jamison didn't listen. He waited, wondering when there was a time when he had waited for anyone.

Finally the woman patted the queer's arm and turned.

'Miss Lawrence,' the President said quickly, 'may I introduce Sherman Jamison?'

The name of Sherman Jamison, one of the richest and most successful tycoons, was well known.

For a moment, an impatient frown clouded Tarnia's face, then she smiled.

God! Jamison thought, what a beautiful smile! What a woman!

She looked at him.

As they exchanged looks, Jamison knew he had not only fallen in love with her, but, by the way her eyes suddenly lit up, she had fallen in love with him.

On very rare occasions when a man and a woman meet, it happens that they immediately know that they have met true partners. This strange chemistry happened to Tarnia and Jamison.

There was a long pause, as they regarded each other, then Tarnia said quietly, 'Nice meeting you, Mr Jamison. I'm sorry I have to leave. I have so much to do.'

Jamison shouldered the gaping President aside.

'I am also leaving,' he said. 'Allow me to drive you anywhere.'

That happened a year ago.

Tarnia commuted from Paradise City to NYC twice a week. In spite of his business commitments, Jamison managed to see her and to dine with her at some discreet restaurant. When in Paradise City, they were even more careful.

Jamison had explained to Tarnia that his wife was a strict RC and, although he had discussed the possibility of divorce, his wife had flatly refused. She was prepared to have a legal separation, but she would not go against the rules of her church and give him a divorce.

Tarnia understood the problem. She knew that by staying with Jamison there could only be disaster, but she was hooked by him. He had a magnetic pull that was too much for her.

Jamison yearned for her. He wanted her to be his constant companion. What a marvellous mother she would make for his future son!

Tarnia refused gently, but firmly, to sleep with him, and this Jamison respected. He knew, unless he married her, this exciting, clandestine partnership must come, eventually, to an end.

Often they sat together in her luxurious five-room apartment in Paradise City: the big picture window looking down on the sea, the palms and the beach. They talked frankly to each other about themselves. To Jamison, it was a joy to relax in her company and to talk about himself and about her.

He had asked her why she hadn't married before now. She was thirty years of age. She told him that marriage and a career didn't mix in her thinking, and Jamison agreed.

'I'm doing well,' she had told him. 'It has been a hard, tough struggle, but I've succeeded. I've had an occasional affair when I was young . . . teenage stuff. Now, most of my work is with the gay boys.' She smiled her brilliant smile. 'No temptation, until you came along.'

Then two weeks ago, he had a shock. They had finished an excellent dinner at a sea-food restaurant, when Tarnia said, looking lovely in the moonlight, 'Sherry dear, we must now face facts. This can't go on. You can't get a divorce. Every time I see you, I suffer.' As he began to protest, she raised her hand. 'Please, listen. This morning I had a telephone call from Guiseppi, the best couturier in Rome. The fashion trend in Rome has enormously increased. Smart, rich women now shop exclusively in Rome. He wants me to be his chief designer. This is a fabulous opportunity. He is offering me an enormous salary and a rent-free apartment if I will go to Rome. He has given me a month to decide.'

Jamison listened, aware that his heart was fluttering uncomfortably.

'Sherry dear, I can't go on like this with you,' Tarnia went on. 'It is tearing me to pieces. I can't even concentrate on my work for I keep thinking of you. So, Sherry, please be understanding. We can't marry, and I must look to my future. I want us to part now. We will have lovely memories, but we must part.'

Jamison had faced many crises in the past, but this one was so unexpected and terrible, for a long moment, he was unable to say anything. Then his hard, ruthless mind moved into action.

'Of course, I understand,' he said, his face expressionless. 'You have a brilliant career before you. Before we make final decisions, there's one question I would like to ask.' He leaned forward, looking directly at her and taking her hand. 'If I were free to marry you, would you be prepared to give up your career, to be the mother of my children, run my homes, go with me on business trips and still remain happy?'

She looked down at their clasped hands for a long moment, then she looked directly at him and smiled.

'Yes, Sherry. I would give it all up, and be happy with you, and I would love to have your children.' She pulled her hand away. 'There it is. It can't happen, so please, please forget me as I must forget you.'

12

Jamison nodded.

'Give me a month,' he said. 'I have a feeling that Shannon is becoming more understanding. I think I could still persuade her. Please give me a month.'

'Sherry, you know you are trying to live in a pipe-dream,' Tarnia said gently. 'Pipe-dreams don't exist. You will not be able to marry me, and I must look after myself. Let's call it a day.'

'Will you give me a month?' Jamison asked, getting to his feet.

She hesitated, then nodded.

'Yes, a month from today, I leave for Rome.'

'Agreed.' He gently touched her face, then left.

As he got into his Rolls, he knew now he had no alternative. He had to arrange to have Shannon murdered.

Lucky Lucan pulled up outside the offices of the *Paradise City Herald*. Although it was past 23.30, lights showed. This was the time when the newspaper was put to bed.

On familiar ground, he made his way up to the fifth floor where Sydney Drysdale could be found in a small office at the far end of a long corridor.

Drysdale was the *Herald*'s gossip columnist. He was a man with his nose and ear to the ground. What he didn't know about the residents and visitors to the City was not worth knowing about. He had five leg-men feeding him continuous information and his scandal column was eagerly read.

With a brisk rap, Lucan opened the door and entered the office where Drysdale was at his desk, contemplating and using a tooth-pick, satisfied yet another column had been filed, and his thoughts were bent on having dinner, then home.

Many times in the past, Lucan had provided tit-bits of scandal, and the two men had a working arrangement.

Drysdale always paid well for any scurrilous information Lucan had to give him.

Drysdale was about sixty years of age, immensely fat, balding, and he reminded Lucan of a big fat slug who had got among the cabbages. Untidily dressed with an open neck shirt, his eyes hidden behind pebble glasses, a dark-veined nose, Drysdale's appearance belied his importance to the *Herald*.

'Hi, Syd,' Lucan said, closing the door.

With exaggerated care, Drysdale focused on Lucan.

'Well, for God's sake! Lucky!' he exclaimed. 'I thought you were in jail.'

Lucan forced a smile. He found Drysdale's sense of humour irritating.

'How's life, Syd?'

'What have you got for me?' Drysdale asked. 'I want to go home.'

Lucan sat down in the visitor's chair, took out his gold cigarette-case and offered it.

Drysdale was known never to refuse anything. He took a cigarette, looked doubtfully at it and then put it into his desk drawer.

'I don't smoke any more,' he said. 'That's a nice case. Who was the old bag who gave it to you?'

'As if I'd tell you,' Lucan said with his charming smile. 'Syd, a favour.'

Drysdale lifted his shaggy eyebrows.

'No favours,' he said firmly. 'If that's all you want, piss off. I'm hungry.'

'Would you be interested to learn that a daughter of one of our rich residents is having an abortion this week?'

Drysdale's fat face brightened. That was the kind of news that fed his column.

'Tell me more, Lucky,' he said, settling his bulk back in his desk chair.

14

'I said a favour.'

'Quid pro quo?'

'You've got it.'

'So what's the favour?'

'I want all the dope you have on Sherman Jamison.'

Drysdale, genuinely startled, gaped at him.

'Sherman Jamison! You must be out of your skull! Now, Lucky, I don't love you, but you are useful. You start getting snarled up with Jamison, and you are certain to land in the slammer.'

'Never mind that. I just want a bit of background information. Tell me about him.'

'Jamison? He's the big shot of the Jamison Computer Corporation, left him by his father. He's tough, ruthless and stinking rich. I would never mention his name in my column. He could buy the *Herald* as you could buy a pack of cigarettes so I leave him strictly alone, as you must. He has a big apartment in New York. A big villa here. He's on first name terms with the President and all the top shots at the White House. He is very VIP and goddamn dangerous.'

Lucan, who was listening avidly, asked, 'How rich?'

Drysdale shrugged.

'Who knows? I would say if you made comparisons, he would make the late Onassis look like peanuts.'

Jesus! Lucan thought, this really is the Big League! This man had come to him and wanted him to murder his wife! A man worth this kind of money!

'Tell me about his wife, Syd.'

Again Drysdale gaped at him.

'His wife? For God's sake, you're not planning to screw her, are you? I know your racket, but that would be strictly for the birds, and could get you into a basket of trouble.'

'Tell me about her,' Lucan said.

Drysdale shrugged.

'Shannon Jamison? She's musical. She runs Jamison's

homes, and she is a strict RC. Not much else to tell you. I doubt if she and Jamison get along. No children. Something always goes wrong when she is pregnant. I do know Jamison is thirsting for a son. She goes to concerts on her own. Jamison is tone-deaf or something.' Again he shrugged. 'As far as I'm concerned, she doesn't make news. No scandal. No boyfriend.'

'Jamison? Does he screw around?'

Drysdale pulled at his short veined nose.

'If he does, it's under the rug. I've had word he sees a lot of Tarnia Lawrence, the dress-designer. Nice piece of tail. In spite of many opportunities, I can't find anything against her. She's a worker and does well.' Drysdale moved his bulk in his chair. 'That all you want?'

And plenty, Lucan thought. Lots to think about. He released his charming smile.

'Fine, Syd. Thanks a lot.' He got to his feet. 'I won't keep you from your dinner,' and he moved to the door.

'Hey!' Drysdale barked. 'Wait a minute. Who's the chick who's having an abortion next week?'

Lucan looked innocently at him.

'One of dozens, I guess,' he said cheerfully. 'I wouldn't know. 'Bye now,' and he was gone.

As Lucan drove back to the Star Motel, his mind was busy.

So a man of Jamison's wealth and stature wanted to be rid of his wife! He was offering two hundred thousand. Lucan snorted. That was chick-feed. He had been seduced by the thought of having such a sum, but he now realized, if Jamison really meant business, it was going to cost him a lot more. Maybe half a million. Lucan hummed contentedly to himself. Now, that was real money! From what he had learned from Drysdale, Jamison couldn't divorce his wife, and he most probably had found a new girlfriend. A tough guy like Jamison wouldn't care what he paid so long as he got his way.

Very VIP and goddamn dangerous, Drysdale had said.

Lucan could believe that. He would have to move cautiously. All the same, by putting such a proposition to him, Jamison could be subjected to subtle blackmail.

Back in his comfortable bedroom at the Star Motel, Lucan took a shower, got into pyjamas and into bed. His mind never ceased to work.

Now, he thought, I have to find a killer. That's the job Jamison is paying me for.

A lethal accident, Jamison had told him. *This has to be utterly foolproof. No police, nothing crude, a convincing lethal accident.*

He considered the few professional killers he had run into in NYC. Crude, no finesse. Then he thought of Ernie Kling. He hesitated. Kling was more than a professional. If Lucan was to believe rumours, Kling had murdered at least twenty unwanted people. He seemed to have a magic touch or more likely a brilliant brain for organization. He had no police record. He lived well in a three-room apartment in down-town Washington. Lucan admitted to himself he was nervous of dealing with a man like Kling. He had met him several times in nightclubs in NYC. They had had a casual drink together. He had sensed Kling's lethal danger. This man was way out of Lucan's league, but he could be the best to swing this deal with Jamison.

After hesitating for sometime, Lucan got out of bed, found his address book, found Kling's telephone number, hesitated again, then put the call through.

Shannon Jamison said quietly, 'The doctor assures me we can have a child. The last four attempts were a freak of nature.'

Jamison stared bleakly across the big, luxuriously furnished room. He was half thinking of Tarnia. He had heard this talk from Shannon until he was sick of it.

17

'Sorry, Shannon,' he said, his voice harsh. 'I want a divorce.'

'But, Sherman, we have gone over this problem again and again.' There was despair in the melodious voice. 'This is not possible. Please don't bring it up again.'

'I want a divorce and a son!' Jamison snarled.

'There is some other woman?'

'Of course! I want a divorce!'

'I am so sorry for you, Sherman. You are nearly fifty. So often men of your age look elsewhere. I have been a good wife and hostess. If you want a separation, I will agree, but it is against my religion to be divorced.'

Jamison turned and glared at her.

'Fuck your religion! I want a divorce!'

Her face white and drawn, Shannon regarded him.

'I hope and pray you don't mean what you are saying,' she said. 'There can be no divorce. Live with your woman. If you want a legal separation, tell me, but there can be no divorce.'

Jamison continued to glare at her.

'You mean that?'

'Sherman, dear, you know I do. Let's go to bed. We could be successful. Come on, my darling, let's try.'

Jamison finished his drink and set down the glass with a vicious clink. His thoughts now were only for Tarnia.

'Bed with *you*? Get out of my sight! I've had enough of this. I want a divorce!'

There was a long pause, then Shannon walked to the door.

'When you want me to go, tell me,' she said quietly. 'I will pray for you.'

Jamison heard the door close softly, then he heard her walk slowly up the stairs.

So vicious was his mood, so frustrated his mind, that he said half aloud, 'Right, you stupid, religious bitch, you've signed your own death-warrant!'

18

2

Ernie Kling bore such a striking resemblance to the movie actor Lee Marvin, that often, gushing, blushing matrons would stop him on the street and ask him for his autograph.

His reply was always the same: 'I only autograph checks,' and, pushing roughly past them, he went on his way.

Kling believed in living in luxury. He had bought a small two bedroom, luxury apartment, down-town Washington, which was his headquarters. He lived like a vicious, hungry tiger, lurking in his lair, waiting for a kill. He had had a long association with the Mafia as an out-of-town hit-man. He would get instructions to go to some city as far as Mexico and Canada, and to waste some man who was being a nuisance. During the years, he had gained a reputation of being utterly professional and reliable. When he did a job, there was no blow-back. The Mafia often steered him to private jobs: a rich woman wanted to get rid of her husband: a rich man wanted to get rid of his blackmailing girlfriend. 'As a favour, Ernie,' a voice would say on the telephone.

Kling would never consider a killing under a hundred thousand dollars, plus all expenses, and as his hit jobs averaged three a year, he could afford to live in style.

He spent his money on clothes and in luxury restaurants. Women didn't interest him. When in need of a woman which was seldom, he made use of a top-class call-girl service. He favoured red-heads, a little overweight, and his treatment of them, as tough as they were, often left them in tears.

Kling had no respect for human life, except his own. Man, woman or child was mere profit to him as long as the price was right.

The black woman who cleaned his apartment, did his laundry and provided dreary lunches made him realize he would have to look elsewhere. He was becoming bored eating out every night. He loved good food, and was one of the fortunates, no matter how much he ate, he never put on weight. He now wanted someone to run his apartment, who was utterly reliable, who wouldn't listen when he answered the telephone, who didn't yak when he was relaxing, and would give him decent meals.

Some eighteen months ago, he had encountered Ng Vee, a starving Vietnamese youth, wearing ragged jeans and a filthy sweat-shirt. The youth had implored him for a hand-out, telling him he hadn't eaten for three days. Kling happened to be in a mellow mood after an excellent dinner and a lot of Scotch. He liked the look of the youth in spite of his dirt. He was of medium height, thin as a stick with big dark, intelligent eyes. Kling made a snap decision and, looking back, he told himself it was one of the best snap decisions he had ever made.

He took Ng to a scruffy Vietnamese restaurant and watched him eat like a starved wolf. Ng kept glancing at him uneasily, not making anything of this tall, lean, grey-haired man, well dressed, and whose tough personality instantly commanded respect.

After eating several substantial courses of Vietnamese food, Ng slowed down. So far this tall man hadn't said a word. He smoked, and studied Ng with probing, slate-grey eyes.

Finally, Ng said softly, 'Excuse me, sir, you are very kind to me, but I am not gay, and I am not on drugs. I just want work.'

'Tell me about yourself.'

Ng's story was briefly told. His mother was a Vietnamese, his unknown father a sergeant in the US army who disappeared when Ng's mother became pregnant. She had made a tiny living selling hot snacks in the Saigon streets. Finally she decided to join the flood of refugees going to the States. By then Ng was sixteen. He had had a certain amount of education and had been fortunate to have been helped by an American RC priest who had taught him to read and write in English. Ng was a bright student, and he had slaved to improve himself. Both his mother and he hoped all would be well when they arrived in the States, but they found the going desperately hard. His mother got a lowly paid job in a Vietnamese laundry. Ng had searched and searched for work, but no one wanted him. After a year of this misery with his mother slaving to feed them both and pay the rent of the one room they had been lucky to find, Ng realized what a hopeless, useless burden he was to his mother, seeing her beginning to starve because she was also feeding him. He knew she would be better off without him. Without telling her, he took to the streets. This was now the third day of his desperate hunt for a job, no matter how menial, and without success. He felt, in misery, he had come to the end of his road.

Listening and watching Ng, Kling decided this youth had possibilities to be moulded into the slave he needed: to run his apartment, look after the chores and be faithful.

'Okay, kid,' he said. 'I've a job for you.' He took out his wallet and produced two one-hundred-dollar bills. He also produced his card. 'Get cleaned up. Buy yourself new clothes and report to me at this address the day after tomorrow at eleven A.M.'

It took Kling only a few days to teach Ng exactly what he wanted and expected. Ng was a rapid learner. He seemed born a natural house-boy, unobtrusive, always on call, keeping in the kitchen when Kling was doing business or talking on the telephone. The apartment was kept immaculate. Then Kling had a call to do a hit job in Jamaica. He would be away three weeks. He had no qualms about

21

leaving Ng to look after the apartment. He explained he wouldn't be back for a while.

Ng nodded.

'No problem, sir. I will take care of your home.'

Kling was paying the boy a hundred dollars a week and all found. When Kling departed, Ng went to visit his mother. He told her of his good fortune and gave her a hundred dollars.

'Make yourself indispensable, son,' she said. 'Take cookery lessons. I will teach you how to wash and iron.'

Seeing the wisdom of this, Ng joined a night class for cookery. His mother taught him how to iron Kling's expensive and fancy shirts. Again he learned quickly. Even with Kling away, Ng never sat in the luxury living-room. He either sat in the kitchen, studying English, or else, in the evenings, watching TV in his bedroom.

On his return, Kling was surprised and pleased to find a hot dinner of an excellent pot roast waiting for him. He was also pleased that his apartment never looked better.

'Say, kid,' he exclaimed, 'you've become quite a cook!'

'Thank you, sir,' Ng said. 'I have taken lessons. Please order what you wish to eat tomorrow.'

Kling grinned.

'I'll leave it to you, kid, so long as it's as good as this.' He took a thick roll of one-hundred-dollar bills from his pocket, peeled off three of them and tossed them onto the table. 'That's for the housekeeping. You fix it.'

'Yes, sir,' Ng said, looking at the tall, lean man with adoring eyes.

When he had cleared the table and was once more in the kitchen, Kling lit a cigarette and relaxed back in his chair. He had got this little bastard hooked, he thought. Man! Was I smart to have picked on him! He's just what I've always hoped for.

A couple of weeks later, he was made to realize just how valuable Ng was to him.

He had gone out with friends for dinner, leaving Ng alone in the apartment, telling Ng he would be back around midnight, and not to wait up for him. That, of course, was unthinkable to Ng. No matter how late Kling was, he always found Ng waiting with coffee ready or an iced drink.

Around half past eleven, the front door bell rang. Ng opened the door and immediately received a violent shove that sent him reeling back.

A thickset man, wearing a shabby sports coat and a greasy hat, came swiftly into the apartment, closing the door behind him. He held a .38 automatic in his right hand.

Recovering his balance, Ng looked at him, his face expressionless.

'Where's Kling?' the man rasped.

'He's out, sir.'

'When's he back?'

'I don't know, sir.'

The man surveyed him and grinned evilly.

'So he's taken to boys now. I'll wait. Get out of my sight. Just keep out of the way, and you won't get hurt.'

'Yes, sir.' Ng eyed the gun and then regarded the man's drink flushed face. 'Before I go, can I give you a drink, sir?'

The man sat down heavily in one of the lounging-chairs that faced the front door.

'Yeah, pansy boy . . . Scotch.'

'Yes, sir.' Ng went to the liquor-cabinet and made a heavy Scotch and soda and added ice. 'Is this how you like it, sir?'

The man took the glass, sipped the drink and nodded.

'Know why I am here, you little cocksucker?'

'No, sir.'

'That bastard Kling killed my brother. So I've come here to put four slugs into his stinking belly. Now get the hell out of here!'

'Yes, sir.' Ng bowed and walked silently into the kitchen.

The thickset man relaxed in the chair and looked around the apartment.

'This motherfucker sure knows how to live,' he thought. 'Okay this is the end of his road. As soon as he walks in I'll give it to him.' He finished the drink and with a vicious movement, threw the glass across the room to smash against the wall. 'It'll be great to see his face when he sees me!'

He sat there for some twenty minutes, then he heard the soft whine of the rising elevator. He stiffened, leaning forward his gun aimed at the door.

A key rattled in the lock, and Kling, relaxed after a good dinner, walked in.

'Hold it, creep!' the man snarled, his gun steady. 'You killed my brother! Now it's your turn!'

Kling was impervious to shock. He moved further into the room and kicked the front door shut with his heel.

'Hello, Lui,' he said quietly. 'Don't get excited.' He eyed the gun in the man's hand. 'This is something we could talk about.'

Lui knew how dangerous Kling was. He grinned.

'No talking, bastard. Here's yours, and may you burn in hell.'

As the gun came up, Kling, knowing he was helpless, braced himself.

Lui couldn't resist the temptation to gloat.

'You never gave my brother a chance. He didn't even know what had hit him. I . . .'

Fingers that felt like steel hooks gripped his wrist. He felt an agonizing pain shoot up his arm that made him yell out. The gun dropped from his paralysed fingers. He felt his arm twist. The steel hooks dug into a nerve which sent pain raving through him. There was no resistance in him. He was dimly aware that his arm was breaking and he screamed.

24

Kling stood motionless, watching.

Ng had crept into the room, silent as a shadow and had come up behind Lui.

Kling made a little grimace as he heard a bone snap. Lui dropped back in the chair, only half conscious, moaning.

Ng picked up Lui's gun. He looked at Kling who was staring with amazement, knowing this slight Vietnamese had saved his life.

'May I kill him, sir?' Ng asked.

Kling's eyes widened with surprise.

'Do you want to kill him, kid?'

'Yes, sir. He insulted me.'

'Well, for God's sake! He'll have to go so if you want to, go ahead. But wait, kid, not here. We don't want a mess in our nice apartment, do we?'

'No, sir. I thought the garage.'

'That's it. Let's take him down.'

Lui was dimly aware of being dragged out of the apartment and into the elevator. Every nerve in his body seemed on fire. He kept moaning, now sightless with pain.

They dragged him into the vast underground garage which housed some three hundred cars.

'This'll do, kid,' Kling said, shoving Lui against a parked car.

'Yes, sir.'

Kling, still slightly bewildered, asked, 'You killed anyone before, kid?'

Ng drew Lui's gun from his hip pocket.

'Yes, sir. Life in Saigon was hard. To learn to survive, I was forced to take care of myself.' He stepped up to Lui who was struggling to stand upright.

Fascinated, Kling watched Ng put the gun barrel close to Lui's temple and pull the trigger. The bang of the gun echoed around the garage. He watched Lui's head jerk back and the thickset body fall.

'Nice shooting, kid,' he said. 'Give me the gun.'

Ng handed the gun to Kling who cleaned it with his handkerchief, then, kneeling by the dead body, he put the gun in Lui's limp hand.

'That's it, kid. Now let's go to bed.'

'Yes, sir. Would you like a drink or coffee?'

Kling burst out laughing.

'Kid! You are really something! You saved my life. That's something I won't forget.'

'You saved my life too, sir,' Ng said quietly. 'That's something I'll never forget.'

As they rode up in the elevator to the apartment, Kling said, 'What did you do to him?'

'Oh, that? A body is full of nerves. You must know where to touch them. Pain paralyses.'

Kling blew out his cheeks.

'So that creep insulted you?'

'Yes, sir. He cast filth on you and on me.'

Kling scratched the back of his neck.

'So you had to kill him, huh?'

'Yes, sir.'

The elevator doors opened and they entered the apartment.

'A drink or coffee, sir?'

'No. Go to bed, kid, and thanks.'

Ng bowed.

'Good-night, sir,' and he went away.

Kling walked to the big picture window and stared down at the heavy traffic far below.

He realized he had not only found a valuable house-boy, but an invaluable partner as cold-blooded and as ruthless as he was himself.

Completely relaxed, Ng Vee lay in his comfortable little bed, staring up at the diffused light on the ceiling from his bedside lamp.

His mind went back eight years when he had lived in the uncertain jungle days of Saigon.

He thought of his mother who had sat all day in the broiling sun on the edge of the kerb, surrounded by various tins containing Vietnamese food, a tiny brazier burning to heat the food when asked for.

Passing peasants, carrying their heavy loads often stopped to eat her food. Often she had as many as ten old, sweaty men squatting in a circle around her. They gave her a few coins in return for a couple of mouthfuls of her food.

When finally she returned to their one tiny room, she was fortunate if she had earned the equivalent of four US dollars. She always retained the scrapings from her various cans for Ng and herself.

At that time, Ng was thirteen years of age, working desperately hard at his studies, guided by the US priest. In the evenings, he would run to the small office of Dr Chi Wu, an aging acupuncture specialist who once had had a thriving practice, but now, because of his shaky hands, was losing his patients.

Chi Wu was eighty-nine years of age: a tiny, wizened man with a long white beard. Ng kept his office and cupboard-like surgery clean.

Chi Wu was lonely and garrulous, and he liked Ng. He often talked to him about his science and, seeing the boy's interest, he expanded, showing Ng the various detailed charts of the human body where the veins and the nerve ends were located.

'There is so much unnecessary bloodshed,' the old man told him. 'A man desires to kill another. What does he do? He uses a gun or a knife. If he had my knowledge he would only have to squeeze this vein or that vein and the man would be dead. In the same way, if a man deserves to be punished, if someone pressed this hidden nerve end, he would experience enormous pain.' He kept pointing to the chart as he talked.

27

Seeing the polite disbelief on Ng's face, he went on, 'Give me your hand.'

Ng did as he was told.

'Here's a nerve here,' Chi Wu said, pointing. 'Now I will very gently press it . . . so . . .'

Ng felt a sharp tingle of pain shoot up his arm and to his brain, bad enough to make him flinch.

'You see? If I had pressed that nerve end brutally, you would have been in agony.'

Ng was fascinated, and listened every evening, extracting knowledge from the old doctor until he was well versed in the science of death-dealing and inflicting pain. It was not morbid curiosity. Ng had a pressing problem and, from what the old doctor was teaching him, Ng realized that his problem could be solved.

For the past three Saturday nights, he found Won Pu, a powerfully built youth, waiting for him as he left the doctor's office. He told Ng to hand over his earnings. The old doctor paid Ng two dollars a week for keeping his place clean. Knowing that Won Pu was capable of doing him a serious injury, Ng complied and, returning home, had told his mother that his earnings had been stolen. She had looked at him in despair. Without his two dollars, how could she go to market and restock her pathetic restaurant?

The following Saturday, he found Won Pu, a brutal grin on his face, waiting. With a quick movement, Ng darted away and made for a long, dark alley. With a roar of rage, Won Pu took after him. Knowing he could easily outpace the bully, once Ng was satisfied that he had drawn his enemy into a dark recess, he stopped. Won Pu came up, snarling.

'Give me the money!' he shouted. 'I will then push your fornicating face into the back of your fornicating head!'

In the dim light of the moon, Ng saw the outstretched hand. His fingers closed on the nerve end and Won Pu screamed, going down on his knees. Ng was on him like a tiger cat, his fingers pressing the vital blood vessel. In seconds, Won Pu was dead.

From then on, Ng had no problems about giving his mother the two dollars he had earned, wondering what she would have said if he had told her how he had rid himself of the thief.

He kept this precious secret of death-dealing to himself. This was so precious, it was not to be shared with anyone.

Twice during the next two years, Ng had been forced to resort to murder to protect his mother from two men, lusting after her. It had been very simple. He had followed each man, pounced in a lonely spot and, without trouble, killed them.

When this thickset man had forced his way into the apartment and had told Ng what he intended to do, Ng knew this man had to be killed. It had been so easy to incapacitate the man, but he understood his master's reluctance to have the man killed in the apartment.

Ng always thought of Kling as his 'master'. There was nothing in the world that he wouldn't do for him.

However, he had shot this man because he didn't want even his master to know of the death-dealing power he had in his fingers.

Having lived with Kling for many months, Ng had come to realize how his master made his money. The fact that his master was a hired killer didn't disturb Ng. It was a way of life, he told himself.

Well, now his master knew that he too was a killer. Who knows? he thought, his master might find him extra useful.

He turned off the light and went peacefully to sleep.

Two nights later, Kling was drinking a brandy after an excellent meal of steak in a cream and pepper sauce, when the telephone bell rang.

He reached out a long arm and picked up the receiver.
'Yeah?' he said.
'Is that you, Ernie?' A man's voice.
'Well, if it isn't some sonofabitch is wearing my shirt.'
A laugh.
'This is Lucky Lucan.'
Kling grimaced.
'Oh, yeah? You're the guy who makes suckers out of old, rich women . . . right?'
There was another laugh at the other end of the line: rather a forced laugh.
'Well, each to his trade, Ernie.'
'So what do you want?'
'You still in business?'
'Sure.'
'What looks like a job has come up, Ernie. It needs looking at in depth. Would you be interested?'
'I'm always interested in making money.'
'What's your going rate now? It's got to be a perfect job, Ernie. Absolutely no blow-back.'
Kling puffed at his cigar. He had little faith in a gigolo like Lucan.
'For that kind of job, three hundred thousand and expenses.'
'Jesus, Ernie! That's high!'
'Sure, but it'd be a perfect job, and that kind of job needs working on. Take it or leave it, Lucky. I've plenty of money, and I don't need the job. Please yourself.'
There was a pause, then Lucan said, 'Okay. I'll talk around. Would you be prepared to fly down to Paradise City in a couple of days, and meet me?'
'Paradise City, huh? That's south of Miami. Sure: all expenses paid, I'll come.'
'I'll see what I can fix. If I get the green light, I'll book you in at the Star Motel where I'm staying. Okay?'

'Sure, but make it for two, Lucky. I have a partner now,' and as Lucan began to protest, Kling, with a jeering smile, hung up.

Charles Smyth was the Jamisons' butler and major-domo. He had been with them since they had married.

Smyth, in his late fifties, was a bean-pole of a man, with balding head, hollow cheeks and a large nose that dominated his features. He adored Shannon and disliked Jamison, who usually ignored him, issuing curt orders from time to time, leaving Shannon and Smyth to run the two homes with the complete efficiency that Jamison expected.

Every morning at exactly 08.00, Jamison came down for breakfast with Smyth waiting. Jamison's breakfast consisted always of orange juice, grilled ham, toast, marmalade and coffee.

'Good-morning, sir,' Smyth said as Jamison came into the breakfast-room. A quick look at the hard face warned him that Jamison was in a bad mood.

Jamison grunted, sat down and began to look at the financial newspapers that Smyth always placed where Jamison could reach them.

Smyth served the grilled ham and poured the coffee. He had watched the gradual deterioration of Jamison's marriage, and it saddened him.

Shannon had left some minutes ago to attend Mass. When she returned, Smyth would consult her about lunch and dinner. He had heard the previous night Jamison's barking voice and, a little alarmed, he had left his sitting-room and listened. He had heard Shannon say: *If you want a legal separation, tell me, but there can be no divorce.* He had hurriedly returned to his room. He believed eavesdropping was an unforgivable sin.

He understood his master wanted an heir. He further understood his mistress had done everything possible. It was a sad and dreadful problem, and Smyth grieved for both of them.

'Smyth!' Jamison snapped as he began to cut up the ham. 'I want a Hertz rental car here at 10.15. Arrange it!'

Startled, Smyth bowed.

'Certainly, sir. Is there anything else you require?'

'No! Arrange about the car,' Jamison snapped and went on eating.

Breakfast finished, he went into his study, carrying the newspapers. Smyth, slightly bewildered, arranged with the Hertz rental service for a Mercedes to be brought to the villa at exactly ten fifteen.

Jamison settled in his desk chair and nodded to himself. This morning, he would meet again this man, Lucan. He was certainly not going to drive up to this man's motel in his Rolls, with the give-away number plates SJ1. He wanted to remain anonymous. He had no idea, of course, that Lucan had made inquiries about him, and now knew who he was. If Lucan didn't come up with a serious proposition, then Jamison told himself, he would shop elsewhere.

As Smyth was clearing the breakfast-table, he saw Shannon's car arrive. He hastily went into the kitchen and prepared Shannon's simple breakfast of orange juice, two slices of toast and cherry jam. He waited a few minutes, then getting in the elevator, went to Shannon's living-quarters that consisted of a large sitting-room, a bedroom, bathroom and a wide veranda, looking onto the sea.

'Good-morning, madam,' Smyth said as he entered the living-room. 'I trust you had a good night.'

Shannon was staring out of the open French windows. She turned, and he was shocked to see how ravaged she looked. He could see she had been weeping. Her face was pale and her eyes dark rimmed.

'Thank you, Smyth,' she said listlessly, and moved to the small table. 'Punctual as ever.'

Smyth set down the tray.

'For today, madam. Lunch? Dinner?'

'No.' Shannon sat down at the table. 'I would like a light lunch, please. A salad or something. We won't be dining in.' She looked up and forced a smile. 'Look after the staff, Smyth, please. I leave you to arrange that.'

'Of course, madam. Then a light lunch for you at one o'clock.'

'Yes, please.'

Smyth moved to the door, then paused.

'Excuse me, madam, but I understand you will be playing the Saint-Saëns concerto tonight.'

Shannon looked up, startled.

'Why yes. It's at a tiny hall. How did you know?'

'If Mr Jamison does not require dinner, madam, I would very much like to attend the concert.'

Again, Shannon registered surprise.

'I didn't know you were interested in music, Smyth.'

'For a number of years, and when it was possible, I have attended your recitals. I have a ticket for this concert. Will it be in order if I attend or will Mr Jamison need my services?'

'He will be dining at his club. Look, Smyth, come with me in my car. You can help me with my cello. Shall we say seven thirty tonight?'

Smyth bowed.

'It will be a great pleasure, madam.' Again, he made for the door, again he paused. 'May I take a liberty, madam?'

She smiled.

'I regard you as the perfect major-domo, and also as a friend. We have known each other for eight years. I have come to rely on you so much.'

Smyth bowed.

'I just wanted to say that unforeseeable things do happen. I would like you to know, madam, that I will always be at your service should you need me.'

33

He bowed again and left the room.

Shannon pushed aside the breakfast-tray and, burying her face in her hands, she began to weep.

Ted Conklin, Jamison's chauffeur, stepped back to admire the Rolls Royce, a large feather duster in his hand.

Conklin had had an extensive course at the Rolls Royce chauffeurs' school before Jamison had hired him. He had been with the Jamisons', like Smyth, since they had married.

Conklin was a short, squatly built man pushing forty-five. He had light sandy hair, a good-natured fattish face, and he and Smyth were good friends. He lived above the five-car garage in a pleasant little three-room apartment and preferred to cater for himself, seldom joining the rest of the staff for lunch or dinner.

He was utterly in love with the Rolls. He spent hours cleaning, polishing, adjusting the engine performance, checking continually the electric controls, knowing all this work was unnecessary, but loving it.

He paid some attention to Shannon's Caddy, and to the Porsche, but there was no love in his work for these other cars, the Rolls had his complete love.

Seeing Smyth approaching, he paused with a final flick of his feather duster, stood back to admire the gleaming coachwork.

'Hi, Charlie,' he said as Smyth came up. 'Isn't she a beauty?'

Smyth was bored with Conklin's adoration of the car.

'Very nice. Does you credit. Mr Jamison will not be needing you this morning, Ted.'

'Isn't he going out then?' Conklin was disappointed. Nothing he liked better than to drive the glittering Rolls along the boulevards, noting the looks of envy from other drivers.

'I've just ordered a Hertz rental car for him,' Smyth said, dropping his bombshell as gently as he could.

Conklin was outraged.

'What for? A rental? What's the matter with the Rolls or the Porsche?'

While crossing the tarmac to the garages, Smyth had also wondered about this odd order. Being astute, he decided that Jamison's two cars which both carried the SJ1 plates were too conspicuous. Jamison was obviously going somewhere where he didn't want to be recognized. He explained this thought to Conklin.

Conklin nodded.

'Yeah. I guess that's about right. Oh well, it's his business. So I have the day off?'

'Yes. He didn't say if he wanted you this evening, so you'd better stay around.'

'That's him!' Conklin scowled. 'No consideration. I could have spent the whole day on the beach.'

'You still could. I will ask him if he needs you to-night.'

Conklin's face brightened.

'Do that, will you, Charlie? Let me know. There's a chick who sells ice cream on the beach who keeps giving me the eye. Something there might develop.'

'Ted, I think their marriage is going on the rocks,' Smyth said quietly. 'Keep this to yourself. I heard him last night demanding a divorce.'

'I've seen it coming for the past two years,' Conklin said. 'A pity. He wants a son. I understand that. Mind you, I like her, and I don't like him, but when a guy has all this loot, he naturally wants a son.'

'She's not going to give him a divorce.'

'I saw that coming too. She being an RC.'

'Yes. I picked up she is offering him a legal separation.'

'That won't get him anywhere. He'll want to find some

other woman who can give him a son, won't he? He'll want to marry her. All nice and ship-shape.'

'That's the problem.'

The two men stared gloomily at the big villa, then Conklin said, 'I can't see Mr J. taking no for an answer. He's a ruthless sonofabitch.'

'Mrs J. is a devout Catholic. He'll have to take no for an answer,' Smyth said uneasily. 'I think it would be best for her to pack up and leave him. Get a legal separation, and let him get on with it.'

Conklin scratched his head.

'Can't see Mr J. standing for that.'

'Look, Ted, you and I have been good friends for eight years. If Mrs J. leaves, I'm going with her. I wouldn't want to stay here with Mr J. Would you?'

Conklin stared at him.

'Go with her? Now, come on, Charlie, you're not thinking straight. What would she need with a goddamn butler? She will move to some small place and play her cello. She won't want you nor me.'

'She'll need me,' Smyth said quietly. 'She'll have plenty of money if that's bothering you, Ted. She'll need someone like you to look after her car and do the garden. I want you to come with me.'

'And leave this beauty?' Conklin turned to stare at the Rolls. 'I couldn't, Charlie. I just couldn't. Anyway, let's wait and see. There could be some other way out which we haven't thought of. Let's wait and see.'

3

At 10.15, Sherman Jamison, a briefcase under his arm, came down the steps of the villa where the rented SE 350 Mercedes was parked.

Smyth was waiting and opened the door of the driver's seat.

'I understand, sir,' he said, as Jamison settled himself behind the driving-wheel, 'that you will not be back for lunch nor for dinner.'

Jamison scowled at him.

'Then you understand wrong!' he snapped. 'Will Mrs Jamison be in for dinner?'

'No, sir. She is playing at a concert.'

'I won't be back for lunch. I'll be back for dinner. Bring me a tray of cold cuts to my study at eight o'clock, and tell Conklin to return this car to the Hertz people on my return.'

Smyth concealed his dismay. He would now be unable to attend the concert, nor would Conklin have a night off.

With a stiff little bow, he closed the car door.

'Very well, sir,' he said.

Jamison drove to his bank.

The teller behind the counter inclined his head as Jamison put the briefcase in front of him.

'Good-morning, sir,' he said. 'What may I do for you?'

Jamison was the Bank's richest and most important client. He always received the red-carpet treatment.

'Put five thousand in one-hundred-dollar bills in the case,' Jamison snapped, 'and be quick about it!'

The teller took the briefcase.

'Certainly, sir.'

He filled out a withdrawal form and gave it to Jamison to sign, then he quickly put the money in the case.

Minutes later, with the briefcase locked in the car's trunk, Jamison drove along Sea Boulevard, turning onto the highway, and at exactly 11.00 he pulled up outside the Star Motel which was the most de luxe of the number of motels built along the beach road, facing the sea.

For the past half hour, Lucky Lucan had been standing outside his motel cabin, anxiously wondering if Jamison had changed his mind. He had taken precautions that he considered necessary should Jamison appear. Hidden, in the motel's living-room, was a tape recorder which was activated at the sound of voices. Lucan told himself that if he was going to get involved in a murder, he must be able to prove that he was only the go-between if the operation turned sour. With a tape of the conversation, Jamison would be as deeply involved as Kling.

He was relieved, although still uneasy, when he saw Jamison pull up outside the motel.

So Jamison was playing crafty, he thought. A hired car. He still imagines I don't know who he is.

He hurried to the car.

'Good-morning, sir,' he said, opening the driver's door. 'Please come in. We can talk quietly, and without interruption in my cabin.'

'We will talk on the ground of my choosing!' Jamison said, his voice harsh. 'Get in the car!'

'But . . .'

'You heard what I said!'

Lucan walked around the car to the passenger's door and sat by Jamison's side. He slammed the door, venting his well concealed frustration that there would be no tape recording.

Jamison set the car in motion.

'Well, sir, I . . .'

'Be quiet!' Jamison barked. 'We'll talk later.'

Man! Lucan thought, this sonofabitch is a real tough cookie. He recalled what Sydney Drysdale had said: *He's VIP and goddamn dangerous*. He found the palms of his hands were damp and he wiped them on the knees of his trousers.

Jamison, his hard, rock-like face expressionless, drove along the beach road, then turned down a narrow lane, leading directly to a vast stretch of sand, sand dunes and the sea.

At the end of the lane there was a turn-around. He pulled up and got out of the car. He surveyed the deserted beach. About a quarter of a mile away where the sand was firm, there were sun-bathers and people swimming in the sea. Their distant shouts faintly reached the two men.

Jamison nodded and got back into the car.

'Now we talk. What have you arranged, Lucan?'

Lucan again wiped his hands on the knees of his trousers.

'I've found the man who will do the job, sir,' he said.

'Who and what is he?' Jamison demanded, turning to stare at Lucan with his cold, hard eyes.

'His name is Ernie Kling. He is connected with the Mafia. When the price is right, he will do private jobs,' Lucan said. 'I've asked him if he is free, and he is. Before taking this further, sir, I thought it best to consult you.'

With blunt-shaped fingers, Jamison drummed on the driving-wheel of the car while he thought, then he said, 'Where is he?'

'He lives down-town Washington.'

'You telephoned him?'

'Yes, sir, but I gave him no details. I told him a job might be coming up, and was he free for the next three weeks. He said he was. So if you want to use him, he is available.'

'How reliable is this man?'

39

'I assure you, sir, you couldn't find a better man for this kind of job. He has worked for the Mafia for years, and there's never been a blow-back. To my knowledge, he has done six or seven private jobs, as yours is. No blow-back. He has no police record. He is utterly reliable.'

'What are his methods of operation?'

'That I don't know, sir. This is not my scene. You will have to talk to him yourself.'

Jamison stiffened.

'I will have nothing to do with him! It is your job to find out his method of operation. You are my go-between. Understand?'

Lucan shifted uneasily.

'It would be more satisfactory if . . .'

'See this man! Tell him what needs to be done, hear what he has to say, then report to me! Is that understood?'

This was something Lucan didn't want. He wanted to put Jamison and Kling together, pick up some money and duck out.

'I thought that if I introduced you to him, sir,' he said, 'I could then withdraw. This is not my scene.'

Jamison glared at him.

'Wrong thinking, Lucan. If you want this money, you are damn well going to earn it. Understood?'

Lucan hesitated, but his greed over-rode his caution.

'I understand, sir. If you want me to act as your go-between, you can rely on me.'

Jamison gave him a hard, sneering smile.

'Right. So it is agreed for two hundred thousand this man will arrange a foolproof lethal accident and you will act as my go-between.'

Here's the crunch, Lucan thought, and licked his dry lips.

'Well, sir, I did ask Kling what his going rate was for a perfect job.' Lucan began to wipe his sweating hands on the knees of his trousers. 'He said four hundred thousand, take it or leave it.'

'You're not trying to be tricky with me, are you, Lucan?' The bark in Jamison's voice made Lucan flinch. 'If you are, you'll live to regret it.'

'I'm telling you what he said. Four hundred thousand and expenses and a perfect job.'

Jamison stared through the dusty windshield at the sea while he thought.

To be rid of Shannon, he wouldn't hesitate to pay a million or even two million dollars. He thought of Tarnia. With her as his wife, giving him a son, how different his life would become!

'What does expenses mean?' he demanded.

'To be a perfect job, Kling will have to stay here for two or three weeks. I would say one or two thousand would cover it.'

'I will pay four hundred and five thousand dollars for a perfect job,' Jamison said. 'No more. Is that understood?'

Lucan drew in a deep breath. This would mean he would clear a hundred thousand for himself.

'Understood, sir.'

'How soon can you begin this operation?'

'I will arrange for Kling to come here tomorrow. We will discuss the operation. I will have his views for you the day after.'

Jamison nodded.

'Then the day after tomorrow, I will pick you up at your motel at eleven o'clock, and we will finalize this.'

'Yes, sir.'

Jamison removed the car ignition keys and handed them to Lucan.

'Unlock the trunk,' he said. 'You will find a briefcase. Take it. It contains five thousand dollars for necessary and immediate expenses.'

41

Lucan relaxed. He was about to ask for money to get Kling to Paradise City.

'Yes, sir.'

He left the car, opened the trunk and took possession of the briefcase.

As he returned to the car, hugging the briefcase, Jamison said, 'Now listen carefully to me, Lucan. Don't ever attempt to play tricks with me.' He leaned forward and, with his thumb, he smeared a gnat that was flying against the inside of the windshield. 'I will smear you like that, Lucan, as I've smeared that gnat. I have a long arm. Remember that.'

Lucan stared into the bleak, cold eyes and flinched.

'Yes, sir. There will be no problem. I assure you.'

In silence, Jamison drove Lucan back to the Star Motel.

'The day after tomorrow at eleven o'clock,' he said.

'Yes, sir.'

Lucan got out of the car and walked quickly to his cabin to telephone Kling.

As Jamison drove up the sandy road that led to the Golf Club, he thought of his meeting with Lucan.

He had expected Lucan would have upped the price, and he wasn't disappointed. In fact, if Lucan had agreed to the original offer of two hundred thousand, Jamison was going to drop him. A man who couldn't strike a bargain was of no use to him.

Well, he thought, the first step forward. Everything now depended on what this professional killer had to suggest. If he didn't come up with a convincing foolproof method of getting rid of Shannon, Jamison assured himself, he could still duck out. Then he thought of Tarnia. She had granted him a month. Time was pressing. He had to be free of Shannon within the month.

As he pulled into a parking slot outside the clubhouse, Jay Wilbur came over.

'Hi, fellow!' Wilbur exclaimed. 'Just the right kind of day for a great game of golf.'

Jay Wilbur was the Chairman of the National & Californian Insurance Corporation. A short, rotund man of Jamison's age, and, although not in Jamison's wealth bracket, he was wealthy enough. He came to Paradise City in the season, mainly to play golf. He and Jamison had known each other for some years and they got along well together. Both men played to +4, and always had an even struggle on the course.

'Hi, Jay!' Jamison said, getting out of his car. 'How goes?'

'Can't grumble.' Wilbur grinned. 'And you: making more money?'

'Can't grumble either. Suppose we have a quick hamburger and get on the course before the rabble?'

Wilbur was eyeing the rented Mercedes.

'Hey! What's this? Where's your super-duper Rolls?'

'My man is doing something to it,' Jamison said curtly, and led the way into the clubhouse.

The bar was deserted. All the members were out on the three courses that surrounded the clubhouse.

As the two men munched their way through a hamburger and drank beer, they talked business. Both of them played the stock-market and they exchanged information.

'We're heading for a hell of a recession, Sherry,' Wilbur said. 'It's bound to come with these new idiots spending and spending on armaments.'

'I guess you're right,' Jamison said. His mind was only half concentrating on what Wilbur was saying. He told himself he would telephone Tarnia sometime in the afternoon and see if she could have dinner with him.

The two men went into the locker-room to change into golfing clothes.

'You'll be at the concert tonight, Sherry?' Wilbur asked as he struggled to put on his shoes.

'Concert?' Jamison paused, zipping up his golf jacket.

Then he remembered Smyth had told him Shannon was playing her goddamn cello somewhere. 'I guess not. Music doesn't interest me. I have a desk-load to work through tonight.'

'Meg and I are going. You know, Sherry, you have a wonderful wife. She is as good as most professionals. We love to hear her play.'

'How's Meg?' Jamison asked abruptly.

He was jealous of Wilbur's three sons.

'She's fine.'

'And the boys?'

Wilbur shrugged.

'Gary will be all right. He's coming into the business next year. He's great, but the other two . . .' He blew out his cheeks. 'Meg tells me to be patient. After all they are only fifteen and sixteen. They do as little school-work as possible, and chase after girls. Charlie is now playing the guitar and looks like a goddamn hippy.'

Jamison picked up his bag of clubs. He thought, when I have a son, there'll be nothing like that. I'll mould my son in my own image. No guitar nor long hair, no chasing girls. I'll make him worthy to take my place when the time comes!

'You're lucky to have three boys. I wish to Christ I had even one!' he said with such savage, heart-felt feeling that Wilbur, startled, looked sharply at him.

'There's time, Sherry,' he said. He knew about the three miscarriages. 'Kids will turn up.'

Jamison grunted and walked out of the locker-room and to the first tee.

Wilbur shook his head as he followed him. A real tragedy, he thought. His wife and he had often discussed the Jamisons' predicament. They were fond of Shannon. Meg had wondered if she shouldn't suggest to Shannon that they adopt a child, but Wilbur wouldn't hear of it.

'You don't make suggestions like that to the Jamisons,' he said firmly. 'This is not our business, Meg.'

The two men didn't play talkative golf. They preferred to concentrate on the game. Jamison found his concentration this afternoon was lacking. He kept thinking of Lucan, and then of Tarnia. He scarcely realized that he was four down at the 9th.

Wilbur said, 'Not on your game this afternoon, Sherry.'

'It comes and it goes,' Jamison snapped and, with suppressed fury, he sliced his next shot into the rough.

Wilbur, seeing how tense Jamison was, didn't say anything. He kept quiet. On the 18th hole Jamison four-putted, and then savagely kicked his ball into a sand bunker.

'Sorry to have given you such a rotten game, Jay,' he said, making an effort. 'Just not in the mood.'

'Well, as you say, it comes and it goes,' Wilbur said, placing his putter in his golf-bag. As he began to move off the green with Jamison, he said, 'Just a second, Sherry. You and I have been good, close friends for sometime. It strikes me you have a big problem on your mind.' Seeing Jamison tense, he went on quickly. 'Anything I can do to help? Meg always says two minds on a problem are better than one.'

Jamison stared across at the golf house, his face expressionless. He wondered how Wilbur would react if he told him he was planning to have Shannon murdered and had already taken a decisive step towards this end. How shocked this fat, kindly man would be! He shook his head.

'A business mess, Jay. Nothing you can do about it. I'll fix it. Thanks all the same.'

'Well, let's go and have a Scotch.'

'Sorry, Jay. I've got this desk-load. I must get back.'

The two men began walking to the clubhouse.

'Will you be free tomorrow, Sherry? I've only one more week here although I'll be leaving Meg to stay on.'

45

'Sorry. No, I'm right up to my eyes. When will you be back?'

'Oh, hell! I was hoping we'd play for at least another five days. I don't know when I'll be back. How long will you be staying?'

'To the end of the month.'

'Will you be back in September?'

'Could be. I'll let you know.'

By this time the two men were in the locker-room. Jamison hurriedly changed.

'I must get moving.' He shook hands with Wilbur. 'I'll be in touch.'

As he hurried away, Wilbur stared after him, a worried frown on his face. He couldn't remember ever seeing Jamison in such a tense mood.

At exactly 13.00, Smyth, carrying a tray, containing shrimp and diced lobster salad, paused outside the door of Shannon's practice room. He listened to the strains of her cello and nodded sad approval. What a tone! he thought. She makes that instrument sing! He tapped and entered, putting the tray on the small table.

'Lunch is served, madam. Perhaps a glass of Chablis or champagne.'

Shannon put down the cello and came to the table.

'No, nothing to drink, Smyth. This looks marvellous. I have a lot of work still to do this afternoon before I feel I can give a good performance.'

As she sat down, Smyth spread a napkin across her knees.

'I understand, madam. You are a perfectionist.'

She looked at him and smiled.

'And so are you, Smyth.'

He bowed and moved to the door, then paused.

'I regret to tell you I will be unable to go with you to the concert.'

46

Shannon, who was beginning the meal, put down her fork and looked up sharply.

'But why?'

'Mr Jamison requires dinner tonight at eight o'clock.'

They looked at each other.

Shannon felt a cold clutch of loneliness. She had looked forward so much to having Smyth with her. To have him greet her after the concert. How good it would have been to have him drive her home and to hear his opinion of her performance.

She felt sick with disappointment: so sick the shrimp and lobster salad became repulsive to her.

'I am very, very sorry, Smyth.'

'I am sorry too, madam,' and, with a bow, Smyth left the room.

Shannon got to her feet and began to move around the large, sunlit room.

This can't go on, she thought. Sherry and I must separate. I know he hates me. I can feel it. My love for him is draining away. Oh, God! Why can't I give him a son? We must separate!

While she was pacing up and down, Jamison was in a telephone booth, talking to Tarnia.

As usual, she sounded a little breathless, but the sound of her voice gave Jamison a great lift.

'How about dinner tonight?' he asked, after their greetings were over.

'Why, yes. I'd love it.'

'Fine! Suppose we meet at the Stone Crab at eight thirty. Would that be all right?'

The Stone Crab restaurant was a small discreet fish restaurant situated some five miles outside Paradise City where neither Jamison nor Tarnia was likely to run into people they knew.

'I'll be there, Sherry.'

'Be seeing you, darling,' and Jamison hung up. He drew in a deep breath. There was much careful thinking to be done. This would be his one and only chance to convince Tarnia that they would soon be able to get married.

He spent the rest of the afternoon in the almost deserted, comfortable lounge of the Athletic Club. He sat in a deep chair in a far corner and no one approached him. He considered his future, thought of Lucan and made up his mind what he would tell Tarnia when they met that evening. Finally, satisfied that he had his thinking right, he went into the Bridge room and played three rubbers with elderly members, playing badly while he kept thinking of Tarnia.

He returned to his villa soon after 20.00.

Smyth had seen Shannon off in her car to the concert, and had prepared a plate of cold cuts for Jamison.

Knowing how anxious Conklin was to have the evening off, Smyth said as he opened the front door for Jamison, 'Good-evening, sir. Do you wish Conklin to return the rented car?'

'No. Tell him to garage the car.'

'Very good, sir. Will you be needing Conklin tonight?'

'How the hell do I know?' Jamison snapped. 'Hasn't he anything to do?' And he started for the stairs.

'Your supper-tray? is ready, sir. Should I sderve it in the study?'

'Supper-tray I'll be dining out!' Jamison barked, and went up the stairs and to his bedroom.

At that moment, Smyth, furious, was about to face Jamison and give his notice. He had had enough of this selfish, inconsiderate man, then he thought of Shannon. As long as she remained, then he would remain. He suppressed his feelings and returned to the kitchen.

Changing quickly, Jamison came down the stairs to the lobby.

'I want the Rolls!' he shouted. 'Hurry up!'

Smyth appeared.

'In two minutes, sir,' he said. 'Will you be requiring me tonight?'

Jamison glared at him.

'What the hell is this?' he demanded. 'You're paid to give service. I may need you. Busy yourself!'

'Very good, sir,' Smyth said, realizing his last hope of rushing to the concert had faded.

A few minutes later, Jamison drove away in the Rolls.

At 20.50, he left the Rolls in a dark place near the Stone Crab, then entered the restaurant to be greeted by Mario, the Maître d'hotel: a short, fat man with a constant smile. Mario immediately recognized Jamison, who had been before.

'My great pleasure, Mr Jamison,' he said.

Jamison nodded coldly. He didn't believe in being familiar with maître d's nor waiters.

'A quiet table for two,' he said.

'Certainly, sir.'

The restaurant only catered for forty people. Each table was so arranged that other diners could not observe their fellow diners.

Mario led the way to a table at the far end of the room, by the big open window, overlooking the sea.

As Jamison sat down, he said, 'As soon as my guest arrives, serve two very dry vodka martinis.'

'Certainly, sir.' With a little flourish Mario went away.

From experience, Jamison knew Tarnia was always late, and that was the reason why he had also arrived late.

At 21.15, Tarnia came to the table. Jamison, seeing her coming, was standing. Their greeting was careful: just smiles and a quick handshake. If there was anyone to report their meeting, it would seem like two people on a business deal.

A waiter appeared and set the martinis before them.

'You arrange everything so beautifully,' Tarnia said. 'It's wonderful to see you again.'

Jamison regarded her. What a woman! he thought. Her white trouser suit with a touch of scarlet at the throat was so chic. Her glossy hair and her beauty seemed to light up the dimly lit restaurant.

'And I can tell you how marvellous it is for me to see you again. I suppose you are very, very busy?'

'As always.' She paused as Mario presented the menus. She scarcely glanced at hers. 'You choose, Sherry.'

'Hungry?'

'Hmm. I've been so busy. I didn't have lunch.'

'Then let's start with crab and go on to the paella. It's good here.'

'Lovely.'

They waited until Mario had gone away, then Jamison said gently, 'You look marvellous, Tarnia. Every time I see you, you pull at my heart-strings.'

She smiled.

'Thank you. And you? You have a marvellous tan.'

'Oh, golf. That's all I seem to do, except business, and think of you.'

The dressed crab was served.

'This looks wonderful,' Tarnia said and began to eat.

Jamison had no appetite. He picked at the food. His mind was concentrating on the moment when he would have to talk seriously to Tarnia.

For several minutes, they ate in silence. Every now and then, Jamison glanced at her, aware that she was a little tense. He waited until the waiter had cleared the dishes, then he said, 'Something up, Tarnia?'

'You always know, don't you?' She leaned back in her chair. 'Yes. I had a telephone call this afternoon from Rome. Guiseppi has invited me to show my collection at his show. It is a marvellous opportunity. He wants me to fly there the day after tomorrow. It's an opportunity too good to miss.'

Before Jamison could reply, the paella was served, he was

grateful for the delay. His mind worked quickly. This could be the solution to the problem that had been worrying him.

'Will you be away long?' he asked.

'At least two weeks. I hope you don't mind, Sherry, but you must see I can't miss such an opportunity. To show my designs to Guiseppi . . . well!'

'It could be longer than two weeks?' He was probing now.

'I suppose it could. I'll fly out with my designs. The actual show isn't until the end of next week. There will be all kinds of things to discuss.'

'Three weeks?'

'Sherry, don't try to tie me down.' She smiled at him. 'Yes, it could even be three weeks.'

Here was the solution! To have Tarnia in Rome when Shannon was murdered was the solution! He had been worrying that Tarnia would be in Paradise City when Shannon died.

He gave her his most charming smile.

'Tarnia, I am delighted. You deserve it! Of course you must seize this opportunity. I'll wait! Don't worry about me.' He leaned forward, smiling at her. 'But you won't sign a contract with this man until the end of this month? That is understood, isn't it?'

'I promised to give you a month to get a divorce,' Tarnia said quietly. 'A promise is a promise.'

'Let's eat. We'll talk later.'

Jamison watched her eat hungrily, merely picking at his own food. He made small talk without really knowing what he was saying. Tarnia responded. She seemed so happy, and he could see her mind often drifted from him to her future triumph in Rome.

The meal finished, they ordered coffee. Both of them lit cigarettes.

'Now, I have news for you, my darling,' Jamison said.

Tarnia looked up.

'Good news?'

'I think so. You did say you would give me a month to be free of Shannon, and we would marry. You did say that, didn't you? You did say that you would give up this promising career of yours to raise my children and run my homes.' He stared at her. 'You did say that, didn't you?'

Did he see hesitation in Tarnia's deep blue eyes?

'You did say that, didn't you?' he repeated.

She looked at him, smiled and nodded.

Was it an uneasy, forced smile? he asked himself uneasily.

'Yes, I did say that, Sherry.'

'Well, here's the good news. Shannon and I have had a long, serious talk. I have finally convinced her of my need for a son. I have told her that I am in love with another woman. Naturally, I didn't tell her who you are, and she didn't ask.' He paused, smiling at Tarnia who had stiffened, and was listening intently. 'I said I understood how she felt about granting me a divorce, but couldn't she see my problem?' He paused to sip his coffee, not looking at Tarnia. 'Then unexpectedly, she told me she would give me a divorce. I hadn't much hope, but that was what she said. She said she might be able to arrange it after she had talked to her priest. In fact, she said, it would be all right. When you return from Rome, my darling, I am absolutely confident our problem will be solved. Be patient. In six months' time, we will be married.' Again he smiled at her. 'But in the meantime go ahead with your work. All I ask you to do is not to sign a long-term contract with Guiseppe. What do you think?'

Tarnia stared down at her untouched coffee. She remained silent while she thought. She loved this man. She wanted to give him a son. Yet, she reminded herself, she was throwing away a remarkable talent if she did marry him. She was excited and elated at the thought of working with the best couturier in Rome. But, she wondered, for how long? With Sherry, her future would be secure.

'Suppose we wait and see,' she said, and smiled at him. 'If and when the divorce comes through, then we can make plans.'

'But, Tarnia, we already know our plans. As soon as I am free, we marry,' Jamison said curtly.

Tarnia looked away from him, then stiffened.

'Do you see who has just come in?' she asked softly.

Jamison, frowning, looked across the restaurant to see Sydney Drysdale of the *Paradise City Herald* lumber in. He was greeted with bows from Mario and led to a table away from Jamison's table.

Drysdale had completed his column and had left it on his desk. Apart from muck-raking, his only other interest was good food. He had decided to have a crab dinner, and what better choice than the Stone Crab restaurant?

'Lots of crab, Mario,' he said, 'and beer.'

'Certainly, Mr Drysdale.' Mario bowed and went away.

Drysdale, his little eyes quizzing, peered at the half concealed tables, always on the look-out for that extra piece for his column.

He saw Tarnia and Jamison and, as he sat down, he thoughtfully picked his nose. Hey! Hey! he thought, well what do you know?

'You don't have to worry about that fat creep,' Jamison said. 'I have him where I want him. Once he printed a smart piece about me. One of his "a little bird tells me . . ." I fixed him good. My attorney told him if he ever mentioned my name again in his rag, he would lose his job. Don't worry about him.'

'He could mention me,' Tarnia said, agitated. She reached for her sling-bag, opened it and took a number of papers from it which she spread on the table. They were receipts and customs papers. 'We are here on business, Sherry. I can't afford any scandal.'

Irritated, Jamison nodded, he picked up some of the documents and pretended to study them, aware Drysdale was watching.

'I'll go,' Tarnia said. 'We shake hands. Stay here for a little while. This must appear to be a business dinner.'

Jamison folded the papers and handed them back to Tarnia.

'Just relax. He won't dare to print a thing about us. I'll telephone you tomorrow. In six months' time, we will be married.'

Tarnia stuffed the papers back into her bag. She didn't seem to have heard what he had said. He could see her one thought was to get away from the restaurant. She stood up, offering her hand.

A quick, business-like hand-shake. The touch of her hand sent a tingle through Jamison, but he kept his face expressionless.

'Tomorrow,' he murmured, then she gave him a quick, impersonal smile and walked out of the restaurant. He sat down and signalled to Mario, who came hurriedly to the table.

'A cognac, Mario,' Jamison said, and lit a cigarette.

Drysdale watched this performance. He was too experienced a muck-raker to be conned.

Well, well, he thought. So S.J. is having it off with the Lawrence piece. Lucky guy! Business dinner! A joke!

Three beautifully dressed crabs were set before him. As he began to eat, he continued to think. Nothing here for me. This rich bastard is too dangerous to write about.

All the same, he told himself, there'll come a time when I'll fix him!

As he finished his first crab and sipped a cold beer, Jamison called for the check, paid, left a handsome tip and walked past Drysdale's table without looking at him, and out to his parked Rolls.

Ernie Kling replaced the telephone receiver and hoisted himself out of the lounging-chair. He walked into the kitchen where Ng was standing over a saucepan which produced an aroma that made his nose twitch.

'Smells great,' he said, leaning up against the door frame of the kitchen. 'What is it?'

Ng smiled at him.

'I think you will like this, sir,' he said. 'It is a national dish which my mother taught me to cook. Saffron rice, tender beef, green peppers and many other herbs.'

'If it tastes as good as it smells, it is okay with me,' Kling said.

'Thank you, sir. I am sure you won't be disappointed.'

Relaxing against the door frame, Kling watched Ng as he stirred the contents of the saucepan. Man! he thought, was I lucky to find him!

'A job's just come up, kid,' he said. 'I'm taking you with me. You'll have fun. We're going to Paradise City, Florida. Loads of sun, sea, swimming. It'll be a real vacation for you, and, maybe, you could help out. Like the idea?'

Ng began to serve the savoury-smelling food onto two plates.

'I am always at your service, sir,' he said.

'Sure . . . sure. But I want you to have a vacation. I want you to enjoy yourself.'

'When I am with you, sir,' Ng said quietly, 'I always enjoy myself. Are you ready to eat?'

Carrying the two loaded plates, Ng went into the living-room and set them on the table.

A real character, Kling thought. He shrugged, then joined Ng at the table.

4

A few minutes before 22.00, Detective 1st Grade Tom Lepski walked into the Detectives' room to find Sergeant Joe Beigler, the doyen of the Paradise City police force, reading through the afternoon's crime sheet, a carton of coffee at hand and cigarette dangling from his lips.

'Hi, Tom,' he said, glancing up.

'Anything for me?' Lepski asked, sitting at his desk. He liked the 22.00 to 04.00 stint. It came around once a week, and there was usually more action during that period than during other stints.

'Nothing for you, Tom,' Beigler told him. 'The usual small time stuff. Mostly kids: car stealing, stealing from shops. Right now, it is quiet.'

Lepski snorted.

'Sometimes, Joe, I wonder about staying in this goddamn city. Here I am, the best detective on the force, and I rarely get a chance to reveal my talents.'

Beigler concealed a grin.

'You never know, Tom. Something could come up, and then you'll be in business.'

'I want a full-blooded killing. I want a snatch. I want a big break-in. Something to get my teeth into.'

Beigler had heard this so often, he winced.

'I'm just going through the unwanted visitors' list. I see Lucky Lucan is in town.'

Lepski released a snort that would have startled a bison.

'That creep! Man! Would I like to nail him! Where's he staying?'

'At the Star Motel. He believes in doing himself well.'

'I would like to put him away for ten years!'

'Look, Tom, don't waste your energy. Lucan has a gold-plated racket. He preys on old, rich women and swindles them. We can't do a thing unless these stupid randy old women make a complaint. Can you imagine them doing that?'

Again Lepski snorted.

'He could slip up. I'm going to watch him. If there's one creep in this city who deserves to be tossed in the slammer, it's Lucan.'

Beigler was getting bored with this. To change the subject, he asked after Lepski's wife. 'How's Carroll?'

'Ah!' Lepski pushed his hat to the back of his head and gave a hoot of laughter. 'I'll tell you, Joe. This afternoon, Carroll said she was going to give me a chicken dinner, but first I had to cut the goddamn lawn and wash the goddamn car. So, okay. I like chicken: finger-licking on the spit: very tasty, but Carroll had found a new recipe. Where the hell she finds these disasters beats me. No chicken on the spit. She was going to treat me to a *real* dinner. She explained the recipe. You cut the goddamn bird into pieces. You put red wine in a saucepan. You add onions and God knows what, then you cook the chicken in this. She said it would be terrific. So, okay, I went along, but I'd rather have had a chicken on the spit. So I cut the lawn and washed the car, while she spent the whole afternoon in the kitchen with the radio going full blast and she singing. I must admit when I went into the kitchen – what a godawful mess it was in – the smell was terrific. Now, I did a stupid thing. We were out of beer and cigarettes, so I drove down and got the stuff. I ran into Max, and we got talking, so I didn't get back for over an hour.' Lepski heaved a sigh. 'Carroll has two big problems. First TV. She will look and watch the little white dots on the screen if the set breaks down. She's an addict. Then she can't resist a telephone call. All her friends keep calling her. So when I get back, Carroll is yakking with some girl friend who is asking her advice about a pain in her tum. If there's one thing that Carroll loves it's talking about health problems. She reads every goddamn woman's magazine published: specializing on the health section. She's known by her friends as Dr Lepski. You ask her: she has the answer. So there's Carroll yakking and smoke coming out of the kitchen.'

'These things happen,' Beigler said who liked Carroll.

'You're right. No chicken dinner. We had cheeseburgers.' Lepski gave a chortle. 'Carroll was upset. I told her to relax. I said, like you've just said, that these things happen. Then I got a shade too smart. While we were chewing these godawful cheeseburgers, I thought I'd try and cheer her up. I said it would be a great idea if I retired from the force, and both of us set up a restaurant. She'd do the cooking, and I'd act as the front man.' He gave a bellow of laughter. 'Well, Carroll fell for this. She asked me if I really was serious. I said we could give it a try, and I had a great name for the restaurant.' Again he became convulsed with laughter. When he had recovered, he went on, 'I said the restaurant should be called "The Burnt Offering".'

Beigler clapped his hand over his mouth to prevent from laughing. Trying to look grave, he said, 'I bet Carroll didn't dig that.'

'You're right.' Lepski again bellowed with laughter. 'The Burnt Offering. Not bad, Joe?'

'How did Carroll react?' Beigler asked, knowing Carroll's temper.

Lepski grimaced.

'Well, you know Carroll. She blew her stack. Another of Carroll's problems is she doesn't share my sense of humour. She stormed out of the house, shouting she was leaving me forever, got in her car and went off like a rocket.'

Beigler, who loved the chance of pulling Lepski's leg, put on a worried expression.

'That's bad, Tom.'

Lepski stiffened, then alarm showed on his face.

'You don't mean she meant it, do you, Joe?'

'Well that kind of joke isn't in good taste,' Beigler said. 'She didn't pack her clothes?'

Lepski came out in a sweat. He wiped his face with his handkerchief.

'She just rushed out.'

'Of course, once she knew you were here on duty, she could be packing and will leave you for good.'

'She wouldn't do that,' Lepski said, mopping his face. 'We love each other.'

Beigler heaved a dramatic sigh and looked mournful.

'Well, Tom, take the advice of an unmarried man. That was a heartless joke. If you don't want to be in the dog-house for months, you've got to placate Carroll. You've got to explain it was a thoughtless joke, and you are ashamed of yourself. Then you back that up with flowers – long-stemmed roses – a big box of candy and a big bottle of her favourite perfume. Do that, and you could just get off the hook.'

Lepski gaped at him.

'Flowers? Candy? Perfume? All that costs money, Joe.'

'Oh, sure,' Beigler said with a smug smile. He loved spending other people's money, 'but then, you've had your fun, so you have to pay for it. Now, Tom, when you come off duty, you drive to the airport and get the stuff and, when Carroll wakes up, she'll find all that luxury waiting for her. Get the idea? You will tell her how sorry you are. My bet is she'll forgive you and she'll cook for you again.'

'Flowers . . . candy . . . perfume,' Lepski muttered. 'Why can't I keep my big mouth shut?'

He got to his feet and, with dragging steps, he left the Detectives' room.

When Beigler was sure he was out of hearing, he exploded into a guffaw of laughter.

'The Burnt Offering!' he exclaimed. 'I love it! This is too good to keep to myself! I must tell the boys! They'll bust their guts!'

In a sour, vicious mood, Lepski drove to the Casino and parked. The Casino was a certain spot where action might happen. He felt in the mood to scare the crap out of the con-men and the card-sharpers who always frequented the Casino at this time. He hadn't long to wait. He spotted Johnny Four Aces, a sleek Italian, whose reputation as a sharper was notorious. Lepski pounced on him and so frightened him, he returned to his car and drove away. Lepski found more successful pounces, scaring away more hopeful sharpers.

Then he saw Lucky Lucan come down the steps of the Casino.

Lepski gave a snort that made the birds in the palm trees flutter up in panic into the night sky. He strode up to Lucan, who was unlocking the door of his rented car.

'What the hell do you think you're doing in this city?' Lepski barked in his cop voice.

Lucan's heart missed a beat. He turned and regarded Lepski. He knew him to be a tough, dangerous cop. This wasn't the time to tangle with him.

'Hello, there, Mr Lepski. Good to see you again,' he said, forcing a smile. 'You're looking well.'

'Don't feed me that crap!' Lepski snarled. 'What are you doing here?'

'Me? Getting a little sun, relaxing, a short vacation.'

'Creeps like you are not wanted here,' Lepski said. 'Take a vacation some place else!'

Lucan pulled himself together. He was sure, during the next three weeks, when he would be working with Kling, he would meet again this bastard cop.

'Is that official, Mr Lepski? You want me to take it up with the Mayor? Now listen, Mr Lepski, until you get a complaint about me, don't lean on me. I don't appreciate it!'

He got in his car, started the engine and drove away.

Lepski watched him go, clenching and unclenching his fists, making a low growling noise that would have done credit on the sound track of a horror movie.

At 05.50, Lepski arrived back home. He took from his car gift-wrapped perfume and a big box of candy, plus twelve long-stemmed roses. He was still horrified at what this junk had cost him. He unlocked the front door, listened, then tiptoed into the living-room. He found a vase and put the roses in it, then put the candy and the perfume on the table where Carroll would see them the moment she came down stairs. He surveyed the scene. It looked pretty good. Well, maybe, he consoled himself, it was money well spent.

'Is that you, Tom, dear?'

Carroll's voice.

Lepski stiffened, then hurried into the lobby. There was Carroll, wearing a see-through night-dress, standing at the top of the stairs.

'Poor Tom, you must be tired,' she said. 'Come on up. Let's go to bed. We have lots and lots of time. Never mind coffee. Come on up!'

Lepski eyed Carroll, thinking she was really the most glamorous girl he knew. In a bewildered daze, he climbed the stairs, and Carroll put her arms around him and gave him a hug.

'Do you forgive me?' she asked. 'I was sorry I got mad yesterday. I'm really sorry.'

'I – I thought . . .' Lepski mumbled.

He was led into the bedroom.

'Take a shower, pet.' Carroll slid into bed. 'Hurry.'

61

Lepski threw off his clothes.

'I should apologize,' he said, 'I . . .'

She burst out laughing.

'Okay, so I was mad. I went to my club and told the girls. They just split their sides. "The Burnt Offering". They loved it. They said it was the wittiest thing they had ever heard, and they are right. You are very clever, Tom. Who else but you would have thought of that?'

'Yeah.'

Still walking in a daze, Lepski went into the bathroom and took a shower. As he stood under the flow of water, he thought of the money he had spent and the gifts downstairs.

But he forgot about that when he got into bed and Carroll wrapped him in her arms.

Ernie Kling lay full length on the comfortable settee in the well furnished living-room of his Star Motel's cabin.

Seated near him in a lounging-chair was Lucky Lucan. At the far end of the room, sitting on a hard-backed chair, was Ng Vee, his expressionless eyes continually watching Lucan.

Kling and Lucan had gone through the chat about the trip from Washington, and how Kling had found Paradise City. He said it looked like his scene.

'Yes,' Lucan said. 'You'll love it. Well, Ernie, money first, huh?' He picked up the briefcase that Jamison had given him. 'I've got you four thousand dollars in cash to cover your immediate expenses.' He had removed a thousand dollars from the briefcase for himself. 'Okay?'

'If it's for *immediate* expenses, I'm not squealing.'

'That's what it's for.' Lucan handed the briefcase to Kling.

Kling said, 'Hey kid, stash this away somewhere safe.'

'Yes, sir,' Ng said and, taking the briefcase, he left the room.

'Who the hell's that chink?' Lucas asked, lowering his voice.

'Don't get your lines crossed, Lucky. He's Vietnamese, and he's my partner.'

Lucan frowned.

'I didn't know you used a partner.'

'I do now, and let me tell you something. He is fifty times the man you are or ever will be. Remember that. Never tangle with him. He's deadly.'

Lucan moved uneasily.

'Okay.'

'Right. Now what's the caper about?'

'A rich man wants to get rid of his wife,' Lucan said. 'She's a strict RC and won't give him a divorce. They can't produce kids and that's what he wants. He's found a woman, and now wants to marry her, so he wants his wife knocked off. That's the story.'

Kling lay still, slightly resembling a deadly snake, basking in the sun, then he nodded.

'Sounds okay. So this creep will pay me three hundred thousand for getting rid of his wife?'

'That's it,' Lucan said, uneasily. 'There are conditions.'

Kling smiled evilly.

'There always are. So . . . ?'

'A perfect job. No blow-back. No cops. A lethal accident.'

'There's never a blow-back when I do a job. Okay, tell this creep I'll talk to him. I'll tell him how I'll handle the job. I'll want information about his wife.'

Lucan blotted his forehead with his handkerchief.

'No, Ernie. He insists on dealing with only me as a go-between. That's the last thing I want, but the deal isn't on unless he deals with me.'

'Why?' Kling asked, now alert.

'Well, he wants to remain anonymous until he is sure you come up with the perfect method.'

'Sort of playing cagey, huh?'

'Yes.'

'Who is this guy, Lucky?'

'I've asked around and through my connections which cost me, Ernie, I . . .'

'Cut out the crap, Lucky!' Kling snarled. 'Who is he?'

'Sherman Jamison.'

Kling sat bolt upright, swinging his long legs off the settee.

'You mean *the* Sherman Jamison?'

'Is there another?'

Kling lay back, lit a cigarette and stared up at the ceiling. He remained motionless for some minutes, then he smiled.

'So Jamison wants to get rid of his wife. Man! Is this a nice, tasty dish!'

Lucan didn't say anything. He waited.

Kling thought, then he said, 'You know this guy's worth billions?'

Lucan licked his dry lips.

'I believe so.'

'Right. He and I are going to meet. This isn't your thing, Lucky. This is between men. You've now got to fix I meet Jamison. You have to find out where he goes so I can meet him. Tell him I need information about his wife. Fix a meeting, then I'll be there instead of you.'

'It won't work, Ernie. He's too smart. He comes here, takes me in his car to a beach to talk. This guy is VIP and very dangerous.'

'So, okay, he's dangerous.' Kling grinned. 'I like dangerous guys. What's he paying you, Lucky?'

'I get a cut off yours,' Lucan said uneasily. 'He's tight about money.'

Kling smiled again.

'So I pay you, huh?'

'I thought ten per cent would be fair.'

Kling burst out laughing.

'You kill me! You're so small-time, I'm almost sorry for you. Well, okay, you tell him I've got a perfect plan cooking, but I need information about his wife. Then fix another meeting. This time I'll take over.' He slid off the settee and walked to the table where he found paper and pencil. He wrote rapidly while Lucan, his heart thumping, watched him. Finally, Kling handed the sheet of paper to Lucan.

'Those are the questions I want answered. Then tell him in two days' time, you'll tell him how I'll get rid of his wife: a perfect job. Fix a meeting, then I'll take over. Got it?'

'I'd rather duck out of this, Ernie,' Lucan said, taking the paper, folding it without reading what Kling had written and put it in his pocket. 'Suppose you pay me off, and you handle Jamison? This isn't my thing.'

As he got to his feet, Kling patted his shoulder.

'Relax, Lucky. You're now in the big league. If you want thirty thousand bucks, you've got to earn it. Run away, and get things fixed. There'll be no problems.'

His hard hand still on Lucan's shoulder, he steered him out of the cabin.

'Bye now,' he said, and shoved Lucan into the hot sunlight.

Ng came from the kitchen.

'I don't trust that man, sir,' he said quietly.

'That makes two of us,' Kling said. 'But he's money-greedy. Let's go take a swim.'

'Yes, sir.'

Changed into swimming-trunks, they walked together to the sea.

'If Lucan gets tricky, we can always fix him, can't we, kid?'

Ng looked up at Kling with an adoring smile.

'Yes, sir,' he said.

The killer and the youth ran into the sea.

Jamison, in the rented Mercedes, pulled up outside the Star Motel at exactly 11.00. He paid no attention to the tall, lean, grey-haired man who was lying on a sun-lounge chair outside a cabin some yards from Lucan's cabin. He was unaware that Kling was studying him behind his black sun-goggles.

Lucan hurried from his cabin and got into the Mercedes.

'Good-morning, sir,' he said, nervously.

Jamison was in a sour mood. He had talked to Tarnia on the telephone, telling her he wanted to drive her to the Miami airport to catch her Rome flight, but she firmly refused.

'No, Sherry. The less we are seen together, for the moment, the better. I'm still thinking of that dreadful man, Drysdale. How I wish he hadn't seen us together.'

'Come on, darling,' Jamison said impatiently. 'Forget him. He knows he dare not print a word about you or me. Well, all right, if I can't see you off, I'll be thinking of you every minute. I understand. And, my darling, when you return, I feel absolutely sure, you will be Mrs Sherman Jamison in six months' time.'

'When you say you are absolutely sure, I believe you,' Tarnia said. 'I'll telephone you as soon as I arrive in Rome. I must go. I have so much yet to do. 'Bye, darling,' and she hung up.

Jamison had replaced the telephone receiver thoughtfully. He was offering to make Tarnia one of the most important, richest women in the world, who would share his life, who would give him a son, who he loved. Yet, her voice had no happy lilt, no enthusiasm. All she was now thinking of was this gaddamn dress show!

So he was in a sour mood when Lucan slid into the car by his side. He said nothing, staring ahead, driving fast, until they reached the beach. Then he stopped the car and turned to face Lucan.

'Tell me!' he barked.

Lucan found he was terrified of this man who was staring at him with hard, ice-cold, probing eyes. God! he thought, how I wish I hadn't got into this thing!

'I've talked to Kling,' he said, his voice unsteady. 'He tells me there is no problem. First, he needs information about your wife, sir.'

'What information?' Jamison demanded.

'He is a perfectionist, sir. When he does this kind of job, there are no blow-backs, but he needs a week at least to study the situation before deciding the best and safest way to do the job.'

Jamison grunted.

'Understood. So . . . ?'

'He needs to know if your wife has any boyfriends.'

'She has not!' Jamison snarled, wishing she had.

'Has she friends she meets regularly?'

'Not regularly, but she has a number of friends, like her, interested in music, who she meets from time to time.'

'Does she have any set routine?'

'What does that mean?'

'People often do the same thing regularly every day: like walking a dog, going to the club . . .'

Jamison nodded.

'She goes to Mass every morning at eight o'clock. She returns for breakfast, swims an hour, then returns to play her cello. Usually, she lunches at home. She is fond of riding. She takes her horse out onto the beach for an hour or so where friends join her. In the evening, she attends concerts or plays herself at concerts. That seems to be her life.'

Jesus! Lucan thought as he scribbled the answers. What a dreary life!

'Is she a good swimmer, sir?'

'Excellent.'

'Rides well?'

'Very well.'

Lucan thought, then he said, 'The hit could be when she came out of church. Would you object to that?'

Jamison stared at him.

'Why should I? She is near to God then, but I can't see . . .' He shrugged.

What a man! Lucan thought. What a savage! What some men will contemplate to get their own way!

'I want a decisive answer by tomorrow, Lucan. If I am not satisfied, then I will drop the project. Tomorrow, at your motel at eleven o'clock. Understand?'

'Yes, sir,' Lucan said, flinching away from this man whom he now regarded as a monster.

Jamison grunted, started the engine and drove in silence back to the Star Motel. He pulled up, nodded, then, when Lucan got out of the car, he drove away.

Kling, still lolling in the sun-lounge chair, got up and walked into his cabin. Lucan followed him.

When the door was shut, Kling asked, 'How did it go?'

Lucan sat down and mopped his face.

'What a swine that man is!' he exclaimed. 'Ernie, I could use a drink.'

Ng appeared out of the kitchen, poured two big Scotches, handed one to Lucan and the other to Kling, then disappeared.

'Take it easy, Lucan. Any creep who plans to have his wife murdered is a swine.' Kling sat on the settee. 'Don't get worked up. Have you the facts I want?'

'Yes.' Lucan handed over his notes, then drank the Scotch greedily. 'I'll be glad to be shot of this! This is just not my thing.'

'Shut your mouth!' Kling said curtly. He studied what

Lucan had written, then nodded to himself. 'You know, Lucky, when people keep to a routine, it is dead easy. No problem here. When do you meet Mr Big again?'

'He's coming at eleven o'clock tomorrow morning.'

'Okay. You take it easy, Lucky. When I need you, I'll call you. From now on, for the next day or so, you're out of the photo. Understand?'

'If you say so.' Lucan got to his feet. 'I leave it to you, Ernie, but don't forget this sonofabitch is dangerous.'

Kling smiled.

'So am I,' he said, and smiled again.

Smyth had seen Shannon return from morning Mass, and he quickly prepared her simple breakfast.

As he entered her living-room, to find her standing before the open French windows, he said, 'Your breakfast is served, madam.'

She turned and smiled at him.

'Thank you, Smyth,' and she came to the table.

'I trust the concert was a great success, madam.'

'I think it was or else people were very kind.' She smiled again. 'Playing before friends is very different from playing before a critical audience.'

'Yes, madam. I understand that. I would have liked to have attended.'

'I know.' She waited until he had poured the coffee, then she went on, 'There was a tape, Smyth. I got a copy for you.' She waved to her desk. 'Take it, and, when you have time, do listen. I value your opinion.'

His face lit up.

'You couldn't be kinder, madam. Thank you.'

He found the tape, bowed and withdrew.

At least, one, real faithful friend, Shannon thought. She spent some time sipping coffee and thinking, feeling in a depressed mood. Friends? she thought. Not *real* friends.

The people she mixed with were so obviously aware that she was the wife of this powerful rich tycoon. They were, of course, music-lovers, but if she had been plain Mrs Joe Doe would they bother to come to the concert hall to hear her play? She thought not. Plain Mrs Doe would be just another amateur cellist. Then she thought of Jay and Meg Wilbur. They were true friends. She recalled their warm congratulations last night. She had known from the pleasure on their faces how much her music had meant to them. Yes, her *real* friends!

She needed so badly to talk about Sherman, and who better than Meg who, she knew, would move cautiously, consult Jay, then give sound advice.

Shannon got to her feet and walked over to the French windows. If she left Sherman, half her way of life would come to an end, but the remaining half could be much more alive. She would no longer be *the* Mrs Sherman Jamison with servants, two luxury homes, no money problems, and with a captive audience to listen to her cello playing. If she separated from Sherman, the snobs would drift away. Although Sherman would have to provide for her, her present life-style would come to an end.

Would she mind? she asked herself.

She felt she needed to talk to Meg before making up her mind. This was a weakness, she told herself. She should be able to decide for herself, but this would be an enormous step.

Still thinking, she undressed and walked, naked, into the bathroom and looked at herself in the floor-to-ceiling mirror. Her reflection gave her confidence. God! If only I could have children! she thought. My body is good enough to keep any man attentive, but not Sherman.

Bitterly, she turned away, put on her swim-suit and went down for her morning swim.

At 07.50, the following morning, Ernie Kling did something he had never done before in his evil life.

Dressed in a dark grey suit, wearing dark sun-goggles, he mounted the steps that led to the Church of the Blessed Virgin, entered the big church and took a seat where he could observe and not be seen.

An altar boy was lighting candles. A concealed organ was playing Bach. Incense hung in the air. There were already a number of people sitting in the front pews: mostly elderly women with a scattering of elderly men.

Kling regarded the scene with cynical eyes. He waited patiently, like a coiled snake. Then he saw Shannon Jamison come down the aisle. He recognized her from Lucan's description and eyed her. Some woman! he thought. He liked her tall, upright figure and the way she moved. With her was a bulky man with flaming red hair who saw her to her seat in a pew, then took a seat away from her.

Kling sat through the service, observing the fat, pleasant-looking priest who officiated. He watched Shannon go up to the altar rails and again nodded his approval.

The service over, Kling still remained seated. He watched the congregation leave, pausing at the doorway of the church to shake hands with the priest. He watched Shannon's smile as she paused for a moment to say something to the priest before moving on. He watched the red-haired bulky man grip the priest's hand firmly and say something, then hurry after Shannon.

Kling got to his feet and walked towards the priest as he turned.

'Fine service, Father,' he said.

The priest regarded him.

'This must be your first visit, my friend,' he said. 'I am good at remembering faces.'

'That's right. I'm on vacation,' Kling said. 'I like to attend church when I can. I don't often get the chance. It's

good to see you have such an attendance. These days . . .'
He shrugged.

'We have our faithful,' the priest said. 'I wish more of the
young would come. We have a better attendance on
Sunday.'

'I seem to recognize that gentleman with the red hair,'
Kling said.

'Mr O'Neil. He is the Irish representative to the United
Nations. He is here for a brief vacation, and attends Mass
every morning. A fine man.'

'Of course.' Kling nodded. 'I have seen his photograph in
the papers. Well, Father, have a nice day.' He shook hands.
'I'll be seeing you.'

'God go with you, my friend,' the priest said.

Stupid, fat old fool, Kling thought as he ran down the
steps to where he had parked his car. He then drove to the
beach where Jamison and Lucan held their talks. At that
hour the beach was deserted. Kling walked around, found
what he hoped to find and then drove back to the Star
Motel.

At 10.30, Lucan came to Kling's cabin. Kling could see
he was in a nervous state.

'Oh, for God's sake, Lucky, relax,' he said. 'Hey, kid,
give this guy a stiff drink.'

'Yes, sir,' Ng said, and quickly produced a double Scotch
and soda.

'Now, Lucky, this is going to be dead easy,' Kling said,
lighting a cigarette. 'No problems for you. All you have to
do is to go with Jamison to the beach. I'll be there. When
Jamison pulls up, you slide out of the car, fast. I'll take your
place. You head for a big clump of shrubs on your right.
The kid will be there, and will take you to where we've
hidden my car. I'll talk to Jamison and sell him my idea.
From what you tell me, he'll fall for it.'

Lucan lost colour.

'I don't like this, Ernie. Jamison warned me he would fix me if I played tricky. With his clout, he will fix me!'

Kling grinned.

'He can't, Lucky. Use what brains you have. What can he do to you? We have him in a squeeze. He knows that if he tries to put the heat on you, you can tell the press he tried to hire you to murder his wife. So okay, he'll deny it. He might threaten to sue, but he won't. Once the press get on to this that he wanted to get rid of his wife so badly he'll pay someone to murder her, he'll never dare get rid of her. So he's stuck with her for life unless he plays along with us. Get it?'

Wiping his sweating face, Lucan nodded.

'I hadn't thought about that. But, Ernie, this is not my thing. I wish I hadn't listened to that sonofabitch.'

'Oh, pipe down! Do you or don't you want to pick up an easy thirty thousand?'

Lucan gulped down the Scotch. His greed overcame his caution.

'Well, okay, Ernie. I'm relying on you.'

'So, do just what I've told you,' Kling said. 'I'll handle the rest.' He got to his feet. 'The kid and I are now going to the beach meeting-place. Just leave it to me.'

When Kling and Ng had driven away, Lucan returned to his cabin. He had another stiff Scotch, then, feeling fortified, and almost reckless, he walked out into the hot sunshine to wait for Jamison to arrive.

5

With Lucan, sitting at his side, Jamison drove towards the beach meeting-place.

Jamison had to restrain himself from asking the vital question: had this professional killer come up with a perfect plan to get rid of Shannon? If he had! His life would be entirely altered. He would have Tarnia, but even more important to him, he would have a son!

He could smell whisky on Lucan's breath. He could see he was unnerved. A gigolo! What could one expect?

He said nothing while he drove, staring ahead, driving carefully. Let this wet gigolo sweat! he thought grimly. If he doesn't deliver, I'll fix him! There are many ways of fixing a gigolo like him. Jamison's fingers tightened on the driving-wheel. If this gigolo didn't deliver, he would hire some thug to smash his handsome face: stamp on him: grind a heel. If he didn't deliver!

He drove the car down the sandy lane leading to the beach, then pulled up.

Now! he thought. Will this be the end of Shannon?

Lucan was waiting for this moment. He was still feeling reckless. As the car stopped and Jamison reached for the ignition key to turn off the engine, Lucan opened the door of the passenger's seat, was out, slightly staggering, and had run frantically to a clump of bushes to his right as Kling had indicated.

For a brief moment, Jamison sat still, then he swung round in his seat to find himself looking at a tall, lean grey-haired man who had appeared from nowhere and had slid into Lucan's seat.

Jamison's nerves jumped and he felt his heart give a little flutter at the sight of this man with his cool, evil smile and his glittering snake-like eyes.

'Morning, Mr Jamison,' the man said, in a soft, low voice. 'I'm Ernie Kling. We have business together . . . right?'

Jamison sat motionless, but his mind worked swiftly. So Lucan and this killer knew who he was. Well, all right, he couldn't have hoped to remain anonymous for long.

Still feeling his heart fluttering, Jamison said, 'I told Lucan I did not want to deal directly with you, Kling.'

'Yeah, he told me, but I don't work that way. If I do a perfect job, I deal with the top shot, not a creep like Lucan. Look, Mr Jamison, if that's not the way you want it, I'll take off. I'll leave regretfully because I have a perfect plan. You want to get rid of your wife. I want your money. This is business, Mr Jamison.'

Jamison thought of being free of Shannon. This man had said: *I have a perfect plan.* He stared thoughtfully at Kling. He had an instinctive feeling this man could deliver the goods.

He said, 'Very well, Kling, tell me your perfect plan.'

Kling smiled.

'Not that easy, Mr Jamison. I don't give away secrets of my trade for nothing. It is understood you and I are now in business? I get rid of your wife without any blow-back, and you pay me three hundred thousand dollars. Right?'

Jamison hesitated, then nodded.

'Yes, that's agreed.'

'Fine. Now how will I be paid?'

'As you like,' Jamison said. 'Cash, gold, you name it, you can have it.'

'I have a Swiss numbered account,' Kling said, taking out a pack of cigarettes. 'How about transferring the money to Switzerland?'

Jamison shrugged.

'That presents no problem.'

Kling nodded. He realized he was dealing with Mr Big who would certainly have banking accounts all over the world.

'Fine. I will want a hundred thousand dollars in my Swiss account before I begin the operation.'

Jamison moved restlessly.

'That's no problem if you can satisfy me you have a perfect plan.'

Kling relaxed back in the car seat and lit a cigarette.

'Okay. I got information about your wife from Lucan. There are several possibilities, but none of them are a hundred per cent safe. For instance, I could fix it she drowned on her morning swim. I could fix it she fell off her horse on her afternoon ride, but these thoughts didn't jell with me. There could be witnesses. You want a perfect lethal death with no blow-back, no cops, so I've dug up another solution.'

Jamison listened to this quiet, hard voice. It came into his mind that he and this professional killer were actually planning to murder Shannon! For a very brief moment, he felt a qualm, then his mind shifted to Tarnia. With Shannon out of the way forever, he would be able to marry Tarnia and have a son.

'What solution?' he asked, aware his voice was unsteady.

'People who have regular routines, Mr Jamison, are easy targets. Probably you don't know that Mr O'Neil, the Irish rep at the United Nations, attends Mass every morning and Mrs Jamison also attends. It seems a regular thing.'

Jamison's fingers began to drum on the car's steering-wheel.

'What has this man to do with your thinking?' he demanded, impatiently.

'Well, Mr Jamison, here is the perfect solution you want,'

Kling said. 'At the end of the service, the priest goes to the church's entrance to shake hands. Mr O'Neil, being the snob he is, goes with your wife. They pause to shake hands with this fat, old priest. At this moment a member of the Irish Republican Army will throw a bomb. Goodbye Mr O'Neil and, more important, goodbye Mrs Jamison. She appears to be an innocent bystander to a political killing. The cops will hunt the bomb-thrower, but won't find him. A nice, clean job, Mr Jamison, with no blow-back. Like the idea?'

'A bomb?' Jamison said, feeling his heart give a lurch.

'Let me explain that, Mr Jamison,' Kling said, lighting another cigarette. 'I am a professional. I've done bomb jobs before. I have access to the new US army's hand-grenade which is completely lethal. All I have to do is to stand across the street, and when I see your wife and O'Neil come out of church I lob the grenade, and that's it.'

Jamison sat back in the car seat as he considered this shocking suggestion.

'But this will be mass murder,' he said, not caring, but for face-saving, making a minor protest. 'A bomb! Some of the congregation and certainly the priest will be killed.'

'Oh, sure,' Kling said, tossing his cigarette butt out of the open car window. 'You want a perfect job, Mr Jamison, so why worry about a fat priest and a few old has-beens who should be dead anyway?'

Jamison thought about the priest, and his fingers tightened on the steering-wheel. This priest was the man who had persuaded Shannon that divorce was against her religion. This priest had poured his slimy, sanctimonious poison into Shannon's ears. Who cared if he died?

He sat still, thinking, while Kling, relaxed and in no hurry, smoked another cigarette.

A political murder! Shannon unlucky to have been among the dead. What an idea! What a perfect plan! Jamison thought of the consternation this bomb outrage would cause among his many friends. How they would rush to send their condolences. He thought of Tarnia, safely in Rome. She would never suspect that he could possibly have had anything to do with this mass murder in which Shannon had died. He would at last be free!

He hesitated no further.

'All right,' he said. 'I agree to your plan. When?'

Kling regarded him. In his evil eyes there was a slight light of admiration. This was a man after his own heart, he was thinking. Some man! Tough, utterly ruthless, not caring a goddamn about how many people died so long as he got his own way.

'As soon as I get a hundred thousand dollars in my Swiss account, Mr Jamison. I've already got the grenade. I just want to hear from my bank that the money has arrived, and on the following morning the job will be done.' He took from his wallet a card. 'That's my account number and the address of my Swiss bank.'

Jamison took the card, glanced at it, then said, 'The money will be in your account the day after tomorrow.'

'That's nice news. Okay, Mr Jamison, you can now leave it to me. On Friday morning, at eight thirty in the morning, you will be a widower.' Kling smiled, opened the car door and got out. Leaning forward, and staring hard at Jamison, he went on, 'You will send the other two hundred thousand dollars to my Swiss bank when you've read the news-papers . . .'

'Agreed,' Jamison said, and started the car engine.

The two men stared at each other for a long moment, then Jamison engaged gear and drove up the sandy lane to the highway.

At midday, Lepski stormed into the Detectives' room and flung himself down at his desk. He tore off his hat and rumpled his hair, then glared at Beigler who had just come on duty and was about to read the night's crime sheet.

Beigler, sensing trouble, regarded Lepski uneasily.

'Hi, Tom,' he said. 'You're early. How did it go?'

'Listen, Joe,' Lepski snarled, 'when next you offer advice, I'll spit in your right eye! Flowers! Perfume! Candy! When I got home, Carroll actually apologized to me! She said she had told her girl friends and they had split their sides, and she was all over me in the sack! Then when we went down to get lunch, she saw the flowers, the perfume and the candy. Okay, I forgot to put water in the vase and the roses looked terrible. She said the perfume was fit only for a hustler and she didn't eat candy as she was weight-watching. Then she flew in a rage and accused me of being drunk last night and squandering money! So, okay, I blew my stack, and we had a row that brought the goddamn neighbours into their gardens to listen. So, from now on, keep your big mouth shut!'

Beigler heaved a sigh, drank some steaming coffee by his side and shook his head.

'I'm sorry, Tom. These things happen.'

Lepski snorted.

'And how come you are always drinking hot coffee? Charlie never bothers to give me any.'

'Well, Tom, it's a quid pro quo.'

Lepski gaped at him.

'Quid pro . . . what?'

Beigler looked smug. In his spare time, he studied a book of quotations and, when the opportunity arose, he trotted out a cliché.

'That's Latin, Tom.'

'Latin, huh?'

'That's right. Translated it means "You scratch my back, and I'll scratch yours".'

Lepski made a noise like a train approaching a dark tunnel.

'Who the hell wants to scratch Charlie's hairy back?'

'Never mind, Tom. I've got a little job for you,' Beigler said. 'Right up your alley. I could have given it to Max or one of the other boys, but I kept it especially for you.'

Lepski regarded him suspiciously.

'Oh, yeah? What job?'

'I have a complaint from the Mayor's office about Lucy Loveheart. According to the complaint she is getting a shade too blatant.'

Lepski's face showed interest.

Every cop, every wealthy resident, every rich visitor, knew Lucy Loveheart. She ran an expensive, de luxe brothel on a side street off Ocean Boulevard. She owned a five-storey house with twelve lush-plush apartments, a vast lounge, a bar, and a black band that provided soft, good swing.

Lucy Loveheart had become a tradition in Paradise City. Born of Russian parents with an unpronounceable name, she had come to the city in her early teens. Her beauty and sexual technique quickly found her rich clients. She saved her money, bought this house and set up a de luxe call-girl service. None of the girls lived on the premises. They came to work when Lucy called them, did what was required of them, received a handsome fee and returned to their own apartments. Lucy's establishment was the acme of discretion.

'What's she been up to?' Lepski inquired.

'The complaint comes from the Mayor's secretary: that prissy old fink who would complain if she saw a dog water a tree,' Beigler said. 'She writes that when passing Lucy's house, she observed an intimate woman's garment out on one of the balconies.'

Lepski pointed like a gun-dog.

'What garment?' he asked.

'I don't know. The old fink didn't say. You'd better go

talk to Lucy. The old fink could cause trouble. Just nice, gentle stuff, Tom. Don't forget Lucy sends us all a turkey and a bottle of Scotch on Thanksgiving Day.'

Lepski put on his hat and got to his feet.

'Right up my alley, Joe,' he said, his good temper restored. 'I haven't chatted to Lucy in months.'

'Don't forget you are a married man, Tom,' Beigler said gravely, concealing a grin.

'Just pipe down, Joe! You talk too much!' and Lepski hurried out of the Station house. He paused long enough to eat a hamburger at Joe's bar, wondering what Carroll was giving herself for lunch, and now wishing he had kept his cool when she started to bawl him out. He hoped, by the time he got home, all would be forgiven, and she would have cooked him an edible dinner.

Leaving his car on Ocean Boulevard, he walked the short distance to Lucy's residence, mounted the marble steps and rang the bell.

The door immediately opened, and Lepski was confronted by a gigantic black, dressed in a purple shirt, black silk trousers, his black shaved head glistening. Lepski knew of him. This was Sam, who took care of the trouble-makers, who vetted all visitors, who was Lucy's right hand.

The black regarded Lepski, then his thick lips peeled into a water-melon grin, showing big white teeth.

'Mr Lepski,' he said and bowed. 'A pleasure, sir.'

'Is Mrs Lucy available, Sam?'

'For you, Mr Lepski, sir,' Sam said, stepping aside. 'It is a mite early, but if you wait a few minutes.'

He conducted Lepski to a luxuriously furnished anteroom.

'Perhaps a drink, Mr Lepski?'

'No, thanks. Tell Mrs Lucy I'm in a hurry,' Lepski said, staring around the room, thinking it must have cost a small fortune to furnish with its antique furniture, the good modern paintings on the walls, the thick Turkish carpet.

'Yes, sir,' Sam said, bowed and withdrew, shutting the door after him.

Lepski pushed his hat to the back of his head and wandered around the room. He didn't like to sit down in one of the antique chairs. They looked as if they could break under his weight.

A few minutes later, Sam appeared.

'If you will follow me, sir,' he said. 'Mrs Lucy will receive you.'

He conducted Lepski to an elevator that silently whisked them to the first floor.

Lucy Loveheart was standing in the doorway of her office, smiling a greeting.

Lucy Loveheart was short and plump with a mass of curly hair, the colour of mashed carrots. She had large violet-coloured eyes, a cupid-bow mouth and an aggressive jaw-line.

She owned to forty-four years of age, although she was actually well into her late fifties.

She was wearing a severely cut coat and skirt and a frilly white blouse and, when she extended her hand, diamond rings flashed on her plump fingers.

'Why, Mr Lepski, how nice to see you. You're looking as handsome as ever, and how is your beautiful wife?'

'She's fine, thank you,' Lepski said and followed her into the big office, furnished with antiques and a big Dali painting dominating the wall behind the desk.

'Have a drink, Mr Lepski,' Lucy said, waving to a chair padded with red leather.

'No thanks, Lucy. This is business,' Lepski said, twiddling his hat and sitting down.

She moved behind the desk and settled herself.

'Business? Well, Mr Lepski, we are both busy.' She smiled. 'What's the business?'

'We've had a complaint from Mrs Hackensmidt, the Mayor's secretary,' Lepski said and grinned.

'That old prune . . . what's her moan?'

'She says when passing your house, she observed an intimate woman's garment hanging from a balcony.'

Lucy raised her eyebrows.

'Extraordinary. What intimate garment?'

'She doesn't say.'

'There are five balconies to my house, Mr Lepski. Which balcony?'

'She doesn't say.'

'Witnesses?'

'She doesn't say.'

'And the police have to waste their time and mine on a stupid complaint like this?'

'Well, she's the Mayor's secretary,' Lepski said with another grin. 'She draws a lot of water.'

'So do I!' The violet-coloured eyes were suddenly hard. 'Forget it, Mr Lepski. I will talk to the Mayor. It's time that old battleaxe was put out to grass.'

'I guess you're right,' Lepski said. 'Just for the record, was there some garment on one of your balconies?'

'Certainly not!' Lucy snapped. 'This is a respectable house, Mr Lepski.'

'Maybe the Mayor won't go along with that,' Lepski said cautiously. 'When we get a complaint, he'll want to know what we've done about it.'

'There'll be no trouble with the Mayor. He'll fix her. Just forget this, will you?'

Lepski nodded.

'I guess you'll be able to handle it. Okay, Lucy. Her letter will get lost.'

For a brief moment, her face hardened as she said, 'And so will she!' Then, getting to her feet, she smiled.

'If you have half an hour to spare,' she said, 'Lulu is upstairs with nothing to do. Would you care for a little fun with her entirely on the house?'

Lepski got hurriedly to his feet.

'Thanks, Lucy, but I've things to do.'

'You poor police officers, how you work!' Lucy patted his hand. 'Anytime when you feel in the mood, it'll be on the house. Sam will fix you up with one of my best girls.'

Lepski, embarrassed, blew out his cheeks.

'Thanks a lot. Well, be seeing you sometime, Lucy.'

The door opened and Sam entered to conduct Lepski to the front door. In a slight daze, Lepski walked back to his car.

As soon as Sam had closed the front door, he took the elevator to the first floor.

Lucy was sitting at her desk, her face like stone.

'Get me the Mayor,' she snarled, her expression vicious.

Recognizing the danger signals, Sam hurried from the room to the small switchboard and dialled the Mayor's unlisted telephone number.

Completely relaxed, Ernie Kling sat beside Ng Vee who drove up the sandy lane and headed for the Star Motel.

At the back, Lucan, sweating, his heart thumping with fear, blurted out, 'For God's sake, Ernie! What happened? What did he say?'

'Stop flapping with the mouth,' Kling snapped. 'I'm thinking.'

It wasn't until he and Lucan were in Kling's cabin, and Ng had given them both drinks, that Kling was prepared to talk.

'Well, Lucky, you've made yourself ten thousand bucks,' he said.

Lucan stiffened.

'You sold him your idea?'

'Of course. I said I would handle it, and I've handled it.'

'What about me? I'm scared of that sonofabitch. Did he say anything about me?' Lucan demanded.

'Don't worry about him. The trouble with you, Lucky, is you've a yellow streak.'

'He's dangerous. So, okay, I'm nervous. I admit it. What's been arranged?'

'Yeah . . . a good question.' Kling stretched out his long legs, enjoying Lucan's fear. 'Now, Jamison is a real hellion. I've worked for lots of mean bastards, but he takes the Oscar.'

Lucan was leaning forward, his eyes wide with apprehension.

'What's the plan, Ernie?' he asked, his voice a little shrill.

'It has to be perfect,' Kling said, paused to sip his drink, enjoying keeping Lucan tense. 'No blow-back. No cops. Not easy. This morning, Lucky, I went to Mrs Jamison's church to case the joint. The whole setup fell into place. Now, relax and listen carefully.' In a soft, hard clipped voice, Kling told Lucan of the plan: the assassination of O'Neil in which Jamison's wife would be involved. The IRA claiming responsibility. Too bad Mrs Jamison was also wiped out.

Lucan listened with growing horror.

'You can't do that!' he gasped, scarcely able to speak. 'A bomb! How about the rest of the congregation? The priest?'

'Oh, sure. I pointed that out to Jamison. A shrapnel bomb would certainly knock off the priest as well as O'Neil and Mrs Jamison. The old fuddy duddies waiting to shake hands would be knocked off too. He thought about this, then shrugged. He could see it was the perfect plan to get rid of his wife. Who cares about O'Neil? The priest? The oldies? He gave me the green light to go ahead, and is

85

paying a hundred thousand dollars into my Swiss bank as an advance. You'll get ten thousand of it.'

Lucan jumped to his feet, his face the colour of tallow, his eyes bugging out.

'No! I won't have anything to do with this! I don't give a damn about the money! You're out of your mind, Ernie! It'll be mass murder! No! No!'

Kling burst out laughing. He lolled back, laughing, while Lucan stared at him in horror. When the laughing fit ceased, Kling straightened, then finished his drink and set the glass down.

'Lucky, you have a brain even a chicken wouldn't envy,' he said, the expression on his face now hard. 'Sit down and listen.'

Lucan was so shaken, he was glad to sit down.

'I said no!' he managed to get out. 'I mean it!'

'Oh, pipe down!' Kling snarled. 'Do you imagine for a moment I intend to kill some twenty people to get rid of a woman who stands in the way of a bastard like Jamison?' He leaned forward. 'But Jamison thinks so. I've sold him on the idea. He couldn't give a damn so long as he is rid of his wife.'

Lucan wiped his sweating face with his handkerchief.

'So you're not going to do it?'

'Of course I'm not going to do it! I've got a hundred thousand bucks out of him. How's that for starters?'

Lucan finished his drink.

'You had me scared. Jesus. I really thought . . .'

'Lucky, you're so stupid it's not true,' Kling said with a snarl in his voice. 'No wonder you chase old, randy women for a living. Do you imagine I would settle for three hundred thousand to knock off the wife of a bastard worth billions? I've checked him out. He's worth at least five billion and has unlimited credit. This deal, Lucky, is worth at least five million to me, and ten per cent to you works out at half a million.'

Lucan stiffened. He felt his mouth turn dry.

A half a million dollars!

'He'll never pay it,' he said, his voice quavering. 'He'll find someone else. You're crazy, Ernie.'

'He'll *have* to pay it,' Kling said and grinned. 'This is not going to be a murder job: it's going to be a kidnap job.'

Lucan felt a tremor of fear run through him.

'Kidnap? That'll bring in the FBI. No, I don't go along with that!'

'This is a chance in a life-time, Lucky,' Kling said. 'I've got it all worked out. It's now up to you. If you want to *earn* a half a million, then you're in, but if you want to chicken out, say so. I can always find someone else for that kind of money.'

Half a million dollars! Lucan's mind reeled at the thought.

'How do I earn it?' he asked, sitting forward and staring at Kling.

'When Mrs Jamison is snatched,' Kling said, 'I want a safe-house somewhere in this city to hide her. Now you know the district. Can you find me a safe-house? That's how you earn the money.'

'I don't have a thing to do with the snatch? I don't have anything further to do with Jamison? All I have to do is to find a safe-house for Mrs Jamison?' Lucas was gaining confidence.

'You read me, Lucky,' Kling said smoothly. 'Maybe some odds and ends for you to help clear up, but that's your big job.'

'What odds and ends?' Lucan demanded suspiciously.

'How do I know? No one earns a half a million without working for it, but you'll have nothing to do with the snatch nor anything to do with Jamison.'

The thought of owning half a million dollars reduced Lucan's fears.

'How do I get the money?'

'As soon as I get the ransom from Jamison, I'll fix it you get your cut. You can have it in cash.'

'Not cash!' Lucan shuddered. 'That's too easily traced. How the hell can I pay all that money into my bank without starting a stink?'

'Have you got a Swiss banking account?'

'No.'

'That's the answer,' Kling said. 'That's how Jamison is going to pay me. He has big assets all over the world. I have an account in a small, private bank in Zurich. I did the Big-shot there a great favour.' He grinned. 'He had been having it off with his secretary and she turned ugly when he found some other piece of tail. So, for free, I got rid of her. A nice little job. She fell off the balcony of her apartment. This guy will do anything for me. Suppose I get him to open an account for you, Lucky? It's secret banking. You have a number. You can transfer money to any country in the world except, of course, USA. How about it?'

Lucan lost all his fears. Man! he thought, I could buy an apartment in Monte Carlo, play at the Casino, not bother ever again with fat, randy old women.

'Okay, Ernie. That sounds great.'

'Yeah, now the safe-house. Any ideas?'

Lucan sat back and thought while Kling watched him. Finally, Lucan nodded.

'I think so. I'll have to talk, but, Ernie, this will cost money.'

'The sky's the limit, if it's really safe for two weeks.'

'It could cost a hundred thousand.'

'So what? We're going to make five million. What's a hundred thousand, and this won't come out of your share. I'll take care of the cost.'

'My prospect is tough, Ernie. She will want an advance.'

'She?'

'I'm thinking of Lucy Loveheart. She runs a top-class,

very discreet brothel. She and I have done business. Whenever I lift a bit of jewellery or something of value, I take it to Lucy and she gives me a fair price. How she gets rid of the stuff I sell to her is not my business. She has around twelve apartments in her house, all fitted to take care of rich lechers, plus girls. At the top of the house is the Whipping room. I just might persuade her to rent it to me for a couple of weeks if the price is right.'

'Whipping room?' Kling said, staring. 'What the hell's that?'

'Lucy deals with all kinds of perverts. There are guys who like to thrash girls, and the more they scream, the better these punks like it, so Lucy has a sound-proof apartment on the top floor. I've seen it. A decent living-room, a bedroom, bath and even a kitchenette. You could let a gun off in there and no one would hear it. What's more there are no windows. Could be your ideal safe-house if Lucy will play.'

'That's a great idea, Lucky. Go, talk to her. I don't give a damn what it costs, but try to get it as cheap as you can. I'll pay ten thousand deposit.'

'Leave it to me, Ernie. I'll go talk to her now.' Lucan got to his feet. 'About my ten thousand. When do I get that?'

'A week, Lucky. It depends on what deal you do with this woman. I'll be running myself short.'

'You'll fix a Swiss account for me?'

'Sure. No problem.'

Lucan relaxed and smiled his charming smile.

'I'll fix it, Ernie,' and he left the cabin almost at a run.

Ng Vee who had been listening to all this from the kitchen came into the living-room.

'Sir,' he said, 'it seems a lot of money to give a disgusting gigolo like that. A half a million dollars!'

Kling stretched his long arms and yawned.

'Who said that creep will ever get the money, kid? What's for lunch?'

After lunch at Chong Wing's restaurant of sweet-sour prawns and side dishes, Lucan, feeling buoyant and fortified, walked up the steps to Lucy Loveheart's residence.

The time was 15.00. With luck, Lucy wouldn't be too busy to see him, he thought, as he rang the bell.

Sam opened the door. Recognizing Lucan, whom he despised, he gave a slight nod.

'Mrs Loveheart,' Lucan snapped. 'It's urgent.'

'I will inquire if she is free,' Sam said, and stood aside. He showed Lucan into the ante-room and Lucan prowled around as Lepski had done some three hours ago. After an irritating wait of fifteen minutes, Sam appeared.

'Mrs Loveheart can spare you a few minutes,' he said and conducted Lucan to the elevator.

Lucy was at her desk which was covered with papers. She looked up, her violet-coloured eyes unfriendly as Lucan entered her office.

'Hello, Lucky. Have you got something for me? We must make it short. I'm busy.'

'When aren't you, dear Lucy?' Lucan said with his charming smile. 'It depends on you how long this will take, but I assure you I'm not going to waste your time.' He sat down in the visitor's chair, crossed his long legs and took out his gold cigarette-case.

'What is it?' Lucy snapped. 'Come on, Lucky! What have you got for me?'

'A lot of money, dear Lucy. Around fifty thousand dollars. Like the sound of it?'

Lucy regarded him.

'You mean you have something you *think* is worth that kind of money?'

'Nothing like that. I'm offering you fifty thousand for a

little service. It'll be in cash,' Lucan said, lighting his cigarette.

Lucy couldn't conceal her surprise.

'*You* are offering *me* money? You must be drunk!'

'Lucy, don't let's waste time. I want to rent the Whipping room for two weeks. I'm offering fifty thousand for the two weeks' rent. How about it?'

Lucy, whose shrewd mind worked quicker than fork lightning, immediately shook her head.

'The Whipping room for fifty? Run away, Lucky. I'm busy.'

Lucan had expected this reaction. He knew Lucy to be very tough.

'Look, Lucy dear, let me explain the setup. A rich client of mine wants to put his wife out of the way for two weeks. She is a little scatty in the head and has caused him a lot of trouble. He just wants to lose her for two weeks so he can do a business deal. He consulted me and I thought of the Whipping room. It's an ideal place to keep this woman. It's only for two weeks. No problem. How about it?'

'Why doesn't he send her to a clinic if she's scatty?'

'Because she isn't scatty enough and wouldn't go. She'll have to be kidnapped, dear Lucy. Now don't get excited. She'll be brought here under sedation. She won't know where she is. You won't be involved. When the time comes for her to be released, she will again be sedated. You won't be implicated, and it will be an easy fifty thousand in your pocket.'

Lucy smelt money. That was something she couldn't resist.

'What you are telling me is a woman is to be kidnapped and hidden in the Whipping room . . . right?'

'That's it.'

'And you're offering twenty-five thousand a week to house her here?'

'Dead easy money, Lucy,' Lucan said, flashing on his charming smile. 'We'll fix it someone will take care of her. You don't have to bother. Just shut off the Whipping room and pick up a nice fifty grand.'

'Kidnapping is a Federal offence,' Lucy said. 'No! Go elsewhere. Run away, Lucky. You're wasting my time.'

'There'll be no blow-back. This woman is scatty. The husband will say she's in a clinic. The cops nor the Feds won't come into it. Come on, Lucy! What's your price?'

'Who is this woman?'

'Don't ask me. I wouldn't know, nor do I care. I'm acting as a go-between. What's your price?'

Lucy thought. There was a long pause.

'Two weeks only?' she asked, staring at Lucan, her eyes hard.

'No more and utterly safe, Lucy. What's your price?'

'For a risky job like this, two hundred thousand,' Lucy said. 'For that I'll rent you the Whipping room for two weeks.'

'That's crazy!' Lucan exclaimed. 'I could easily find some place else, but I wanted to do you a favour. Look, let's say sixty a week. How's that?'

Then began the haggling. After twenty minutes, Lucan, now sweating, agreed the sum should be one hundred thousand a week with a ten thousand cash down-payment. As it wasn't his money, he didn't really care. He promised to let Lucy have the down-payment by tomorrow and she agreed the Whipping room would be closed to clients as soon as she had the deposit.

Feeling a little limp, but triumphant, Lucan got in his car and drove fast to the Star Motel.

It so happened that Lepski, sitting in his car, brooding about Carroll, had spotted Lucan as he drove past in his rented Mercedes. Because he hated Lucan, Lepski decided to follow him. He was surprised to see Lucan enter Lucy Loveheart's residence. He had waited and saw Lucan leave. He wondered what a gigolo like Lucan was up to in Lucy's brothel.

6

When Jamison had left Kling, he drove up to the highway and headed towards the city. The heavy traffic irritated him. He wanted a long pause to think, so, at the next layby, he pulled in and cut the car engine. He leaned back in the car and lit a cigarette.

A shrapnel bomb!

This man Kling was a true professional! Who would have thought of such a perfect solution but a true professional?

He nodded to himself. An ingenious idea! No one would suspect him. At that early hour of 08.30, when the service would be over, there would be few, if anyone, passing the church. Kling was a professional. He was sure either to disguise himself or to make certain not to be seen when he threw the bomb.

Not for one moment did Jamison consider those people who would be wiped out as they stood in the church doorway, shaking hands and listening to the priest's blessing.

He thought about Kling. That lean, evil face! Jamison was sure that, given the money, Kling would rid him of Shannon.

On Friday morning, he would be free! He would telephone Tarnia in Rome and gently break the news that Shannon was no more. He would tell her of what a terrible shock it had been to him that this brutal assassination had happened, involving Shannon.

Thinking, looking back, he now regretted not calling in a professional killer long before this. Next month, he would be fifty years of age, which was not the best time in a man's life to raise a family, but, he thought, better late than never.

Friday!

He then thought he would be faced with forty-eight hours before Kling went into action.

The thought of spending these long, tense hours under the same roof as Shannon, knowing she would be dead on Friday, became unthinkable.

No!

He decided he would fly to NYC on the excuse of urgent business. That was the solution, he told himself. He would be in his New York office when the bomb exploded. He would rush back to Paradise City, but during the inevitable delay the police would have cleared up the remains. He hoped he wouldn't have to identify Shannon, shattered by shrapnel. He would return as the stricken husband.

He looked at his watch. The time was just after 13.00. There was a flight from Miami to New York at 15.30. He set the car in motion and drove fast to his villa.

As he pulled up, he saw Conklin dusting the Rolls.

'You are to drive me to the airport in half an hour,' he barked. 'Then return this car to the Hertz people.'

As he entered the lobby of the villa, he found Smyth waiting.

'Pack me a bag: no tuxedo,' he snapped. 'I am leaving for New York. I will be away until Friday afternoon,' and he walked into his study.

'Perhaps lunch, sir?' Smyth asked.

'Nothing! I am leaving for New York in half an hour!' and Jamison slammed the door.

There happened to be some unimportant business that he could discuss with his directors. It would provide an excuse to break his vacation. He got the files from his drawer and put them in his briefcase. His mind was now only on

Tarnia, far away in Rome. The mother of his future son! He longed to telephone her, to tell her, that by Friday he would be free to marry her, but he knew this would be too dangerous. He must contain his impatience. When Shannon was dead . . . then was the time!

A tap on the door made him look up, scowling. Then Shannon entered the room and closed the door behind her.

The last person he wanted to see! Staring at her, he had to admit she was beautiful, and he felt an odd sick qualm run through him to think this beautiful woman, by Friday morning, would be blown to pieces.

'Ah, Shannon . . .' he said, forcing a smile.

'I want to talk to you,' she said. 'Am I interrupting something?'

He lifted his hands in a gesture of bogus despair.

'I'm afraid so. I have this merger coming up, and I am leaving for New York immediately.' He was irritated to hear how husky his voice sounded. 'I'm sorry, Shannon. I have a lot on my mind.'

'I too have a lot on my mind,' Shannon said quietly. She didn't come further into the room, but stood, looking directly at him. 'I want to discuss it with you. I have decided we can't go on living like this. I want a legal separation.'

He regarded her, his eyes cold. A separation? Well, yes, they would be separated forever on Friday morning, but not the way she was thinking.

By Friday, this wife of his, asking for a legal separation, would be dead!

'I must go,' he said, getting to his feet. 'We will discuss this Friday night. I'll keep Friday night clear. Let's have dinner together here, and we'll talk about the future. You will want to know how you stand if you leave me, won't you?'

She studied him for a long, uncomfortable moment and

Jamison was dismayed how his heart fluttered and his hands turned clammy.

He was thinking: there will be no dinner and no discussion. By Friday morning, you will have no future to discuss with me.

'Very well, Sherman, then Friday night,' she said. 'I won't keep you,' and, turning, she left the room.

Jamison took out his handkerchief and wiped his damp hands.

Smyth tapped and entered.

'The Rolls is waiting, sir. I have your bag.'

Jamison found he had to make an effort to get to his feet. He found he lurched slightly as he walked by Smyth. He hoped he wasn't going to have further trouble with his heart condition which his doctors had assured him was only due to overwork. This last and forever meeting with Shannon, knowing she would be dead very soon, appeared to have made a bigger impact on his ruthless nerves than he had bargained for.

He paused in the doorway, stiffened his shoulders, then walked steadily down the marble steps to the waiting Rolls.

Lucan found Kling lounging in the sun outside his cabin. The time was 18.00.

Kling raised his hand as Lucan, smiling, sank down on a lounging-chair by his side.

'Did you fix it, Lucky?' Kling asked.

Lucan had been given Jamison's five thousand dollars, plus another five thousand dollars, supplied by Kling, to pay Lucy Loveheart's deposit. He had seen her, handed over the money, and had been given the key to the Whipping room.

'No problems, Ernie.' Lucan handed the key to Kling. 'That's it. I've done my stint. It's now up to you. You have the room for two weeks. When will you pay her?'

'Don't worry your head about that,' Kling said. 'I'll fix it.' He smiled. 'I'm a great little fixer.'

Lucan became alarmed.

'Ernie, for God's sake, don't try to double-cross Lucy. She's tougher than teak and she draws big clout in this city. You're not planning . . . ?'

'Oh, relax, Lucky. She'll get her money.'

'How about *my* money?' Lucan demanded, sitting forward. 'Have you fixed my Swiss account?'

Kling flicked ash off his cigarette.

'We haven't got the ransom yet, have we?'

'But you'll fix it?'

'Sure. Just relax. You're almost within reach of a half a million,' Kling said. 'That should give you sweet dreams.'

'*Almost?*' Lucan's voice shot up. 'What do you mean? Our arrangement was as soon as I found you a safe-house, I'd get the money. What's this "almost" thing?'

'Look, Lucky, I have first to case the joint.' Kling regarded the key Lucan had given him. 'I'll have an unconscious woman on my hands. I have to get her up to this room, and it's got to be done fast and smooth.' He got to his feet. 'So you and I will go take a look at the setup. I want to know the lay-out.'

'There's no problem,' Lucan said, beginning to sweat. 'There's an underground garage. You drive in. You'll see an elevator on your left. You go up to the top floor. You have the key. No one will see you. That's it, Ernie.'

'Sounds great,' Kling said. 'Okay, let's take a long look, huh?'

An hour later, Kling, who had surveyed the scene and was satisfied, patted Lucan on his shoulder.

'Okay, Lucky. You've done a good job. Now, you stick around. I may need you. Just stay within reaching call,' and he walked into his cabin, firmly closing the door.

Ng was waiting. He came into the living-room.

'I have prepared curried prawns and a mixed salad for dinner, sir,' Ng said. 'Would that please you?'

'Great.' Kling sank into one of the lounging-chairs. 'Give me a drink.'

When Ng had given him a Scotch, Kling regarded him.

'Are you any good at lifting a car, kid?'

'You mean steal a car, sir?'

'Yeah.'

Ng nodded.

'No problem, sir.'

'Right. Tomorrow morning at six, I want you to get a car and bring it here. Take it from some over-night car park. Together, we'll handle this kidnap job. It'll be dead easy. The woman goes to church at seven thirty. The plan is to stop her as she leaves.' Kling sipped his drink. 'I want you to cope with her. I want her unconscious. Can you fix that, kid?'

Ng nodded.

'Yes, sir. No problem, sir.'

Kling laughed.

'There are times, kid, when you kill me. Nothing's anything of a problem to you, is it?'

Ng stared at him, his eyes bewildered.

'Should it, sir?'

'Okay.' Kling shrugged. 'Suppose we eat? Smells fine.'

Five minutes later, the killer and his slave were eating a big dish of curried prawns with rice, fried bananas and red peppers.

'Kid, you certainly know how to cook!' Kling said as he shovelled food into his mouth.

'Thank you, sir.'

'How would you like to own half a million dollars?' Kling asked abruptly.

Ng paused, his loaded fork hovering before his mouth while he stared at Kling.

99

'A half a million dollars? Who wants all that money?'

Kling ate some more, then said, 'Money buys a hell of a lot of fun, kid. With half a million tucked up your jersey, you could live well, you wouldn't have to slave for me, you could have girls, you could have a ball.'

Ng made a little grimace.

'I wouldn't like that, sir. If you are offering me all this money, I thank you, but I don't need it. I want to be with you. I don't need money.'

What a character! Kling thought.

'How about your mother, kid?'

'Perhaps if you would let me have no more than three thousand dollars, I could make her more comfortable, but no more.' Ng ran his fingers through his thick, black hair. 'My mother is difficult, sir. She thinks I am a houseboy, working for you.' He looked up and stared earnestly at Kling. 'And that's what I am. I want her to be sure of that, sir. I can tell her you won a big bet and insisted on giving me three thousand dollars, so I give it to her. That she would accept. She is difficult.'

Kling shrugged, then pushed away his chair.

'Okay, kid. That was a great meal. Tomorrow at six o'clock, I want a car here. We'll drive to Jamison's villa and pick up the woman. Got it?'

'Of course, sir,' Ng said, and began to clear the dishes while Kling wandered over to the TV set and turned it on.

Arriving at the La Guardia airport, Jamison took a taxi to the Waldorf-Astoria hotel where he was received with bows and smiles.

On the flight up, he had decided not to return to his NYC apartment, although there would be servants there to look after him. The apartment would hold too many lingering memories of Shannon who had made it one of the most luxurious, comfortable homes he had ever lived in.

100

It was too late now to go to the office. He would go there in the morning for a brief visit before returning to Paradise City.

Sitting in the comfortable living-room of the hotel suite, he sipped a vodka martini which the waiter had served. His mind shifted to Tarnia. He had an irresistible urge to talk to her. Glancing at his watch, he calculated it would be 01.00 in Rome. She would be in bed, but, he was sure, glad to hear his voice.

Picking up the telephone receiver, he told the operator to connect him with Miss Tarnia Lawrence at the Excelsior Hotel, Rome.

A twenty-minute wait tore at his nerves. Finally, the operator told him that Misss Lawrence had checked out that morning and had left no forwarding address.

Jamison felt a spasm of frustrated rage as he slammed down the receiver.

What was happening? Where had Tarnia gone? Then he remembered that this bloody couturier had told her he would lend her an apartment. She must have moved there!

He finished the martini and poured himself another from the big cocktail shaker. He looked at his watch again. The time was 19.00. In less than fourteen hours, Shannon would be dead and he would be free!

Then he remembered that as soon as the bomb had exploded, the police, Smyth, his friends, would want to contact him. It would take a little time before the news hit the headlines of the newspapers.

He snatched up the telephone receiver and told the operator to connect him with his villa in Paradise City. After some minutes' delay, he heard Smyth's voice: This is Mr Jamison's residence.'

'Any messages for me?' Jamison barked.

'No, sir.'

'I am staying at the Waldorf-Astoria for the night,'

Jamison said. 'I will be returning on the four o'clock flight. Tell Conklin to meet me at the airport.'

'Certainly, sir.'

'We will be dining in, Smyth. Prepare a decent dinner. Is Mrs Jamison there?'

'No, sir. Mrs Jamison left half an hour ago. I believe she is attending a concert.'

Thank God for that! Jamison thought. To have to talk to Shannon would, he felt, be too much for his jumping nerves.

'If anything important turns up, you can reach me at the hotel until 09.30. Then at my office.'

'I understand, sir.'

Jamison hung up.

That takes care of that! he thought. Now what was he going to do? He thought of those bleak hours ahead of him. The club? The thought of talking to his various friends with this thing hanging over him was impossible. A movie? A woman? Impossible!

If he could only talk to Tarnia, he felt sure he would be able to relax. Tomorrow, he must find out the telephone number where she was staying.

Getting to his feet, he began to pace around the room. Tomorrow at eight thirty! Another twelve hours!

He remembered he hadn't had lunch and although not feeling hungry, he rang room service and ordered a plate of chicken sandwiches and another shaker of martinis. He continued to pace, thinking of Tarnia until the waiter brought the sandwiches and shaker. He poured himself another drink and ate two of the sandwiches. As he continued to pace up and down, a thought dropped into his mind that made him pause.

Just suppose Tarnia changed her mind about giving up her career and marrying him. Just suppose this couturier had persuaded her to remain in Rome. The thought brought him out in a clammy sweat. He remembered Tarnia's lack of enthusiasm when he had said, as soon as the divorce went through, she would become his wife. Had he imagined this? No! This was dangerous and stupid thinking! He was sure she loved him, sure that she wanted to give him children.

If I'm going to spend the night in this state, I'll go out of my mind, he told himself.

Sleeping-pills!

That was the answer! Oblivion until the morning when Smyth or the police would tell him Shannon was no more and he was free.

Forcing his mind to remain blank, he undressed, took a hot shower, then four sleeping-pills which he always travelled with. His usual dose was one pill, but he wanted to be sure that he would sleep through the night. Getting into bed, he turned off the light.

In the dark, his mind came alive again. Suppose the temptation of continuing her brilliant career would prove too much for Tarnia. He was so much older than she was. Suppose she met a man of her own age, and he interested her, sharing the same talents. Suppose . . . suppose . . .

The sleeping-pills took charge of him and he drifted off into a heavy, dreamless sleep.

The persistent ring of the telephone bell by his bedside brought him awake. For a few seconds, he didn't know where he was, then his razor-sharp mind clicked into action. He looked at the bedside clock. The time was 08.55.

This was it! Here was the news that he was longing to hear! Shannon was dead and he was free!

He threw off the bedclothes, swung his feet to the floor and snatched up the receiver.

The hotel operator said, 'Your butler, Mr Jamison, is asking to speak to you. I hope I didn't disturb you.'

God! The way these creeps sucked up when you had money! Jamison thought, then snapped, 'Put him through!'

There was a click, then Smyth said, 'Mr Jamison?'

'Yes . . . yes! What is it?'

'Mr Jamison, I have very bad news for you,' Smyth said, and Jamison could hear Smyth's voice was shaking.

'What is it?' he barked, thinking, so at last I am free to marry Tarnia!

'I fear Mrs Jamison has been kidnapped,' Smyth said. 'It would certainly appear so.'

Jamison's heart skipped a beat, then began to pound. *Kidnapped!* What was this old fool drivelling about? Maybe he was trying to break the news that Shannon had been blown to pieces by a bomb.

'Kidnapped?' he shouted. 'What are you talking about?'

'Perhaps, sir, I should tell you what has happened.'

'For Christ's sake, tell me!'

'Well, sir, Mrs Jamison left here for church at her usual time. Conklin observed her driving down the drive until he lost sight of her at the bend. At eight thirty, he walked down the drive and found Mrs Jamison's car parked in the middle of the drive, near the gates which were closed, but Mrs Jamison was not in the car. Conklin telephoned me from the lodge and I immediately joined him. I found a piece of paper under one of the windshield-wipers.'

'Get on with it!' Jamison snarled.

'On this paper, sir, was a typewritten message. I have it here,' Smyth said, huskily.

'Get on with it, for Christ's sake!'

'Yes, sir. The message reads, "Jamison, your wife has been kidnapped. If you want to see her alive, don't alert the police nor do anything smart until you hear from us at eight o'clock tonight". That's all, sir.'

In his long life, Jamison had faced many tricky situations. His mind, trained over the years, was geared to cope with emergencies.

'Right, Smyth!' he snapped. 'Do nothing! Understand?

Move the car back to the garage and wait for my arrival.' He had so often travelled to and fro from Miami to New York he knew the flight schedules by heart. 'I will catch the eleven-thirty flight. Tell Conklin to meet me at the airport,' and he hung up.

It would be a race to catch that flight. Without bothering to shave or shower, Jamison scrambled into his clothes, refusing to think what had happened. It wasn't until he was seated in the aircraft, taking off for Miami, that he surveyed the situation.

A gyp!

He realized he had been double-crossed. His fists clenched. This is what comes, he thought, of dealing with a Mafia crook! Kidnapped! So now the price would be enormous. Well, he thought, I have all the money in the world, and I will pay, so long as I am certain that I will be free of Shannon. Any money paid out would be worth my being free!

The air hostess brought him a flacon of coffee. While he was drinking the coffee, his hard, ruthless face creased into an unpleasant smile.

Jamison, he told himself, you have been out-smarted. You stupidly led with your chin, and you've taken a sock, but not a knock-out sock.

He remembered a cliché so often used by his father: *He who laughs last laughs best*. Okay, Mr Kling, he thought. I'll fix you, and I'll fix that stinking creep, Lucan. First, I must examine the scene. I am not Sherman Jamison for nothing!

Then he thought of Tarnia. There would be no telephone call to her to tell her he was free. His mind shifted to the note that Kling had left in the car: *If you want to see her back alive, don't alert the police*. The last thing he wanted was to see Shannon alive. All the same, he must keep the police out of this. First, he must know what ransom Kling would be

105

demanding. He thought of Smyth and Conklin. He would have to convince them that he knew what he was doing. They were stupid, but devoted to Shannon, but he felt certain he could overawe them.

He poured himself another cup of coffee and relaxed back in his seat, his mind busy, as the plane winged him back to Miami.

Lepski sat at his desk, his eyes clock watching. In another ten minutes he would sign off and go home. He had promised Carroll to take her to a movie and then out to dinner. Why women wanted to be taken to some stinking movie and then eat out when it was much more comfortable sitting at home defeated Lepski, but that's the way women are made, he told himself.

He was thumbing through a book of comics, having had a dull, uneventful day, when his telephone bell rang.

Reluctantly, Lepski lifted the receiver.

'Charlie here,' a voice told him. 'I've a kid who wants to see the best detective on the force, so I thought of you.' Charlie Tanner was the desk sergeant whose job was to sort out the goats from the sheep, and also supply Beigler with coffee. 'Do you want to see him?'

Lepski looked at his watch. The time was now close on his checking-out time: 18.00.

'What's he want?'

'He says he has an important statement to make, but he won't talk to anyone but the best detective on the force.' There was a suppressed gurgling sound as Charlie Tanner smothered a laugh. 'Do I send him up?'

'What are you sniggering about, Charlie?' Lepski snarled. 'If this kid wants to talk to the best detective on the force, then goddamn send him up,' and Lepski slammed down the receiver.

The boy who walked up to Lepski's desk was around ten

years of age, remarkably fat, well dressed with a moon-shaped face, ornamented by big glasses.

'You Mr Lepski?' he demanded, his voice surprisingly confident.

'That's me,' Lepski said, pushing his hat to the back of his head. He always made a habit of wearing his hat when at his desk. He imagined it gave him a tough, movie-like appearance.

'The fink downstairs said you were the best detective on the force. Right?' the fat boy said.

Lepski smirked.

'That's a fact, sonny. So what?'

'I want to make a statement about a serious crime.'

'Is that right? Now look, sonny, I'm busy. What do you call a serious crime?'

'Kidnapping,' the fat boy said.

Lepski gaped at him.

'Kidnapping? What are you talking about?'

'That's a serious crime, isn't it?'

'Sure. Kidnapping, huh?' Lepski lifted his hat, scratched his head and replaced his hat. 'Now listen, sonny, if you're wasting my time, I could make it rough for you. Are you serious or are you trying to be smart?'

The fat boy regarded Lepski with bored eyes.

'Do you want my statement or don't you? I have to get home for dinner. If I'm late, my father moans. If there's one thing I hate more than another it's when my father moans.'

'Okay. Sit down and tell me,' Lepski said, pushing his hat further back. 'Who was kidnapped, when and where?'

The fat boy looked around, pulled up a chair, settled his bulk on it and rested his chubby hands on his still more chubby thighs.

'To save time, shouldn't you get out a form, know who I am, where I live, and then take my statement?'

Lepski made a noise like a buzz-saw hitting a knot of wood.

'My father makes noises like that,' the fat boy said. 'He has digestive problems.'

'Yeah.' Lepski produced a pad from his desk drawer. 'Okay, sonny. What's your name?'

'Frederick Whitelaw, and I would be glad if you didn't call me "Sonny". My friends call me Fat-ma, but you're not a friend.'

Lepski began to drum on his desk.

'That's right, Freddy Whitelaw, huh?'

'Yes. My father is Hubert Whitelaw who owns the Whitelaw chain of self-service stores,' the fat boy said complacently.

Lepski became attentive. Hubert Whitelaw was one of the more important citizens of Paradise City.

'Yeah,' he said, and wrote on his pad. 'You live at Villa Verbena, on Ocean road . . . right?'

'That's where I live.'

Lepski wrote the address down.

'Okay. What's this about kidnapping.'

The fat boy stuck his forefinger up his right nostril, moved it around, but found nothing to interest him.

'I am a bird-watcher, Mr Lepski.'

Lepski leered.

'I'd have thought you were a bit young to start that.'

The fat boy sighed.

'Feathered birds, Mr Lepski. The ones that fly. Not those who would interest you.'

A real smart little alec, Lepski thought, drumming his fingers on his desk.

'So you're a bird-watcher, huh?'

'Yes. Every morning at seven, I climb a tree in our garden. I've built a hide up there, and I watch birds. I see all kinds of birds: mocking-birds, cardinals, painted buntings . . .'

'Okay, okay,' Lepski interrupted. 'I have the photo. What's this about kidnapping?'

'This morning, at a few minutes to eight o'clock, I was in my hide and saw Mrs Sherman Jamison kidnapped.'

Lepski reacted as if he had been goosed by a red-hot iron.

'*Mrs Sherman Jamison?*' he bawled, half starting out of his chair.

The fat boy nodded complacently.

'That's right. They live across the road. Snobs. I've no time for them. They're too rich.'

'You saw Mrs Jamison kidnapped at eight o'clock this morning?' Lepski said, speaking slowly and distinctly.

'That's correct.'

'How do you know she was kidnapped? Now listen, Freddy, if this is your idea of a joke, you'll be sorry.'

The fat boy stuck his forefinger up his left nostril and still found nothing to interest him.

'I can't do more than tell you, can I?'

Lepski's mind began to race. Sherman Jamison's wife kidnapped! Jesus! This would set Paradise City right back on its rich heels!

'Okay, Freddy. So what happened?'

'I was in my hide. Looking across the road, I saw a car pull up right outside the Jamisons' gates. A man got out and lifted the hood as if the car had broken down. This interested me, so I watched.' The fat boy regarded Lepski. 'Are you getting all this down?'

'Not yet,' Lepski said, controlling his temper. 'Keep going.'

The fat boy shrugged.

'Okay. So I saw Mrs Jamison drive down to the gates. She always goes to church at this time. Because this other car was blocking the gates, she got out of her car and walked to the driver to ask him, I guess, to move his car out of the way. While they were talking, a little guy came out of the stalled car and caught Mrs Jamison around the throat. She collapsed. This little guy carried her to the stalled car, threw her in the back, and the two of them raced off. It took less than half a minute.'

'Right,' Lepski said. 'The time, according to you, was before eight in the morning. Now here you are reporting this incident at 18.00. Ten hours after this happened.'

The fat boy nodded.

'Yes. I was sitting for an important exam. I couldn't get to you before. I spent all day in the exam room, then I had to walk to you.'

Lepski suppressed a snort.

'Okay, Freddy. Exams are more important to you than a kidnapping, huh?'

'They sure are. I have to look to my future.'

'I get the point. So you saw two men kidnap Mrs Jamsion. Tell me about these men.'

'I was in my hide. It wasn't easy to see much of them. It happened fast. One of them was tall and thin. The other was small and thin. Both were wearing big sun-hats so I couldn't see their faces. I was looking down on them, but I did get the number of their car.'

'That was smart of you,' Lepski said. 'What's the number?'

'PC 766880.'

'Hold it a minute.' Lepski snatched up the telephone. 'Charlie?'

'Who else?' Tanner growled.

'Trace car number PC 766880 fast!'

'That number rings a bell. Hang on.'

Lepski drummed on his desk while he waited, then Tanner said, 'That car was reported stolen early this morning.'

'Who owns it?'

'The Reverend Owen.'

'Car been found?'

'Not yet.'

'Okay, Charlie, put out an emergency alert. We want this car found, and when it's found it's to be impounded for fingerprints. It could be a kidnap car. Okay?'

'So at last we're in business,' Tanner said. 'Leave it to me,' and he hung up.

The fat boy was listening to all this and he nodded his approval.

'You sure are the best detective on the force,' he said. 'Can I go now? I'll be late for dinner.'

'You'll have to stay a while, Freddy. Do you want to call your parents?'

'I guess I'd better.'

'Okay. Now, listen, Freddy, if this is a kidnap job, don't say a thing. Understand? Tell your dad you have met friends and you won't be home.'

The fat boy frowned.

'How about my dinner? I'm hungry.'

'I'll fix that,' Lepski said, containing his impatience. 'How about a nice juicy cheeseburger? I'll tell someone to bring it to you.'

'I'd rather have a double hamburger and plenty of onions.'

Lepski felt his blood pressure rise. He snatched up the telephone receiver.

'Charlie! Send up a double hamburger with lots of onions and, for God's sake, don't make a thing of it!' and he slammed down the receiver.

While the fat boy telephoned his home and explained he wouldn't be back for dinner, Lepski listened, ready to snatch the receiver from him if he said the wrong thing, but the fat boy's performance was convincing. As he hung up, he said, a little sadly, 'My ma doesn't really care. My pa cares less.'

'That's the way the cookie crumbles, Freddy,' Lepski said, suddenly sorry for this fat boy. 'Now, let's get down to business.'

Lepski listened to the boy's description of the two kidnappers: one wearing a white suit, the other wearing a T-shirt and dark-green slacks. More than that he couldn't say.

Mrs Sherman Jamison, the wife of the richest and most powerful man in the city, kidnapped! The FBI would have to be notified, but first Chief of Police Terrell who was probably in his garden, tending his roses. Then Beigler must be notified. He regarded the fat boy uneasily. If this kid was conning him! But he didn't think so.

'Look, Freddy, you are quite sure all this is the truth?'

'I'm telling you,' the fat boy said impatiently. 'You don't have to believe me. Where's this hamburger? I'm hungry.'

Lepski drew in a deep breath and picked up the telephone receiver. In minutes, he was reporting to Terrell.

'I'll be right down,' Terrell said. 'Keep the boy with you,' and he hung up.

A patrolman came into the Detectives' room, carrying a plastic sack.

'Someone here wants a hamburger with onions?' he asked, an injured look on his face.

'Give it to him!' Lepski snarled, waving to the fat boy. 'And take that stupid look off your stupid face!'

The patrolman dropped the sack onto the fat boy's lap and beat a hurried retreat.

Lepski telephoned Beigler, knowing he was probably drinking coffee and watching the games on the television.

The news Lepski told him made Beigler grunt with dismay.

'I'll be right down. The Chief know?'

'He's on his way,' Lepski said, and hung up.

The fat boy was beginning to munch one of the hamburgers.

Lepski suddenly remembered that Carroll would be waiting for him to take her to a movie and then to dinner. He looked at his watch, then released a moan. Snatching up the telephone receiver, he called Charlie Tanner.

'Charlie! Call Carroll and tell her I have an emergency and won't be able to take her out tonight. Call her right away!'

'Not me!' Tanner said. He knew only too well of Carroll's explosive temper. 'I want to keep my right ear-drum intact. You call her.'

'You heard what I said!' Lepski yelled. 'Call her or I'll tear your liver out!' and he slammed down the receiver.

The fat boy, his mouth full, nodded his approval.

'You are sure the best detective on the force, Mr Lepski,' he mumbled. 'Boy! That's telling him!'

Ten minutes later, Chief of Police Fred Terrell, a big, burly man with sandy hair, strode into the Detectives' room. He took the fat boy into his office and listened to the account of the kidnapping, making occasional notes.

'That's fine, Freddy,' he said, when he was satisfied the fat boy had nothing further to tell him. 'You have been most helpful. I am now relying on you not to say anything about this to anyone. It is vitally important when dealing with kidnappers to keep them guessing.'

'Mr Lepski told me that,' the fat boy said. 'Okay.'

'Thank you. Would you like to be driven home in a patrol car?'

The fat boy shook his head.

'No, thanks. My folks don't expect me back so I guess I'll go skating.'

'Good idea.' Terrell, who had a soft spot for children, not having any of his own, took out his wallet and produced a ten-dollar bill. 'Suppose you have a feed before you go skating?'

'Sure will,' the fat boy said, his eyes glistening. 'Thanks.'

JAMES HADLEY CHASE

When he had gone, Terrell called in Lepski and Beigler.
'Looks as if we have a kidnapping in our laps,' he said.
'I'm sure the kid was speaking the truth. It's now close on
eleven hours since Mrs Jamison was snatched. The chances
are Jamison has already received a ransom note. The fact he
hasn't reported to us indicates there was a threat not to
contact us. That doesn't mean we do nothing. The first
move is to contact Jamison and get his reactions.'

Terrell reached for the telephone and asked the operator
to connect him with the Jamisons' residence.

114

7

At 08.30, Ng Vee drove the stolen car down the steep ramp that led to Lucy Loveheart's underground garage.

Kling sat by his side. Shannon Jamison's unconscious body lay on the floor of the rear of the car, covered with a rug.

'I'll take a look,' Kling said as Ng pulled up by the elevator door. He slid out of the car, checked no one was in the garage, then nodded to Ng. He went swiftly to the elevator and pressed the down button.

'Move fast, kid,' he said as the elevator door swung open.

Ng opened the rear door of the car, grasped Shannon's ankles and pulled her out of the car. He caught hold of her, lifted her, his right arm around her limp body, his left hand under her knees.

'Want help, kid?' Kling asked.

'Oh no, sir. No problem.'

Ng carried Shannon to the elevator, entered and leaned against the wall as Kling got in and pressed the up button.

Holding Shannon, feeling her scented hair against his face, feeling her round, firm breast in his right hand, and her soft thighs under his left hand, Ng experienced a sensation he had never known before.

During his teenage life, he never had the money to associate with girls. His mother had warned him girls were always expensive, and to keep away from them. Ng had found this no hardship. There were times when he felt the stirring of sex within him, but because of his way of life and his mother's repeated warnings, he had crushed down this

115

urge and, up to this moment, women had meant nothing to him.

The sensation he now experienced as he held Shannon's limp body against him gave him an extraordinary feeling of pleasure. It was during the elevator's climb to the top floor, without realizing it, Ng fell in love with Shannon Jamison.

Kling was speaking, and Ng had to force himself to concentrate on what his master was saying.

'Will she be okay, kid?' Kling was asking. 'She looks knocked out.'

'Oh yes, sir,' Ng said. 'In less than a couple of hours, she will be fine.'

The elevator door swung open. Kling moved forward, checked there was no one around, then stepped across the corridor and, using the key Lucan had given him, unlocked the door of the Whipping room.

'Get her in here, kid, and fast.'

Holding Shannon closely against him, Ng carried her through the open doorway and into the big, luxuriously furnished bedroom. He crossed to the bed and laid her gently down. He stood back, feeling his heart thumping.

'Okay, kid,' Kling said. 'You stay with her. I'll get rid of the car. Take a look around. When she comes to the surface, tell her she's been kidnapped and she has nothing to worry about. I don't want her to start flipping her lid. Get the photo?'

'Yes, sir.'

'I got Lucky to stock the refrigerator,' Kling went on. 'She'll be here for at least a week. Look after her, kid. Lucky also bought clothes for her. They're in the closet. She's to have the VIP treatment. Jamison might be tricky, and I don't want her complaining if we release her.'

Ng stared at him.

'But you *will* release her?'

'It depends on Jamison. Don't worry your head about

that. You can leave all that to me.' He handed the key of the apartment to Ng. 'Lock her in when you leave, and come back to the motel dinner-time.'

'Yes, sir.'

'Okay. I'll get rid of the car. Take a taxi back to the motel. Look after her, kid. No rough stuff for the moment.'

'No, sir,' Ng said huskily.

'You're great, kid. I'm relying on you,' and Kling left the apartment.

When the door closed behind him, Ng turned and regarded Shannon as she lay on the bed. She was wearing a white, simply cut dress and it had rucked up, revealing her long legs and shapely thighs.

Ng moved forward and gently adjusted the skirt of the dress. He stood for some minutes looking down at her. What a beautiful woman! he thought, and again this sensation of sex and love moved through him. He felt he could stand there and look at her forever, but he made an effort and turned away. He went into the tiny kitchen and inspected the refrigerator which was packed with *Quick frozen meals*. He grimaced. Dreary food, he thought. He found a coffee percolator and two sacks of ground coffee. He inspected the bathroom and found towels and soap.

Then he returned to the bedroom and sat down in a lounging-chair, close to the bed. He watched Shannon, and waited, with oriental patience, for her to recover consciousness and as he watched her, his love for her grew.

He thought of Kling. He had asked Kling if he would release this unconscious woman.

It depends on Jamison. Don't worry your head about that. You can leave all that to me.

He thought of what Kling had done for him and his mother. He had long ago realized that Kling's way of life was influenced and directed by and for money.

117

Ng drew in a deep breath.

Money? What was money?

All his life up to now, money had meant nothing to him except to buy food. Yet money seemed everything to Kling.

Ng moved restlessly.

Would Kling be so money crazy that he would kill this beautiful woman if her husband wouldn't give him the money he was asking for?

Would he? *Could* he?

Ng again looked at Shannon. She now appeared to be sleeping.

He got to his feet and, for the first time in his life, he did something that set the blood moving through him and his heart pounding.

He gently lifted her hand and kissed it.

As Kling drove up to his motel cabin, Lucan came rushing out of his cabin. He caught hold of Kling's arm as Kling got out of his car.

'What happened?' he demanded. There was sweat on his face and his eyes looked wild.

Kling regarded him with contempt.

'Oh, for God's sake, relax!' he said. 'It went as planned: as smooth as silk. She is now safely in the knocking-shop, and the kid is looking after her.'

Lucan moaned with relief.

'I've been waiting and flipping my lid,' he said. 'Anything could have gone wrong!'

'Not with me handling it,' Kling said. 'I'll see Jamison tonight, and get the money out of him.'

'Suppose he won't pay?'

Kling gave a sneering laugh.

'He will. I have him over a barrel. Take it easy, Lucky. I'm taking a swim.'

Lucan began to unwind.

'You really mean this is going to work? I'll get half a million?'

'That's it, Lucky. It's really going to work.'

'Have you fixed this Swiss account for me?'

Kling gave Lucan his evil smile.

'I can't do anything like that until Jamison pays up. Take it easy. I'll fix it.' Then shoving by Lucan, he went into his cabin and slammed the door.

Lucan returned to his own cabin.

A half a million dollars! he thought. Could he trust Kling? Once the money was in Switzerland, he would pack up and leave America. He would settle probably in Monte Carlo. He paced the room, thinking. God! How he wished he could go now!

He paused by the window to watch Kling, wearing swim-shorts, running down to the sea: his tall, lean body moving with perfect rhythm.

The time was nearly 09.00. Lucan went into the kitchenette and heated up coffee. Kling had said he wouldn't be seeing Jamison until tonight. As he sipped the coffee, he thought of the long hours ahead. Kling seemed so sure he could handle Jamison. Could he? Jamison was a tough, ruthless sonofabitch!

Then he became aware that someone was knocking on his cabin door. Frowning, he put down his coffee-cup, went to the door and opened it. He was shocked to find himself facing the fat, balding Sydney Drysdale of *The Paradise City Herald*. The last person he wanted to see!

'Hi, Lucky,' Drysdale said with his fat, oily smile. 'I was passing so I thought I would look in.'

'Sorry, Syd,' Lucan said, his voice shaking. 'I – I've got a date. Some other time, huh?'

'Who was that tall, lean tough you were talking to?'

Lucan felt sweat start out on his face.

119

'Oh, that guy? I don't even know his name. He lives down the way.'

'Is that right?' Drysdale was watching Lucan sweat. 'Tell me, Lucky, how did you make out with Mrs Sherman Jamison?'

If Drysdale had punched him in the face, Lucan's reaction couldn't be more evident. He started back, his face turning a waxy white.

'I don't know what you are talking about,' he gasped. 'See you sometime, Syd,' and he tried to close the door, but Drysdale's enormous bulk held the door open.

'Oh, come on, Lucky,' he said. 'I'll keep it under the wraps. Have you screwed her yet?'

'Get out!' Lucan screamed hysterically. 'Get out!'

Drysdale smiled.

'A little disturbed, Lucky. Unlike you. See you,' and he moved back allowing Lucan to slam the door.

Heavily, Drysdale plodded back to his car. He settled himself, lit a cigarette and did some thinking.

Something was cooking, he told himself. Years of experience to smell out scandal sent red lights flashing in his shrewd, cunning brain.

Why was this stupid gigolo in such a panic? Why had he reacted so violently when Shannon Jamison's name was mentioned? Who was this tough-looking man Lucan had been talking with?

Loose threads, but Drysdale was an expert at knitting loose threads together.

He started his car and drove back to his office.

Jamison arrived at his villa in Paradise City at 17.45. He had been met at the airport by Conklin. Jamison, his face hard and set, got into the Rolls and snapped to Conklin to get him home fast. He wasn't talking to a bird-brain like Conklin.

Smyth was waiting in the lobby and, with a jerk of his head, Jamison indicated he was to follow him into the study.

Jamison sat behind his desk while Smyth, looking old and pale, stood before him.

'Give me this kidnap note!' Jamison barked.

'It is on your desk, sir.'

Jamison looked around, found a scrap of paper, studied it, then pushed it aside.

'You have followed my instructions? You have said and done nothing?'

'Yes, sir. I have said nothing about this terrible kidnapping,' Smyth said, his voice trembling. 'I have had six telephone calls from Mrs Jamison's friends. They were all asking if she was going to the concert tonight. I told them she had migraine, and couldn't be disturbed.'

Jamison nodded.

'That was efficient of you, Smyth.'

'Thank you, sir, but Mrs Clayton has been twice on the telephone. She wanted to come here, but I managed to persuade her that Mrs Jamison didn't want to be disturbed.'

Jamison scowled.

Meg Clayton, Shannon's best friend! Always a bloody nuisance!

'These kidnappers could be amateurs, Smyth,' he said. 'They could panic and murder Mrs Jamison. They say their ransom demand will be made at eight o'clock tonight. In the meantime, I will handle any telephone calls for Mrs Jamison, and there is to be no leak about this damnable situation. Understand?'

'Of course, sir.'

'Can Conklin be relied to keep his mouth shut?'

'Yes, sir.'

'Very well. Leave me!'

'Sir, I am very sorry about this. You can rely on me . . .'

Smyth began, but Jamison waved him away with a savage gesture of impatience.

When Smyth had left the room, Jamison sat at his desk for the next twenty minutes, staring into space, his mind active. He kept thinking of Tarnia. Not for a moment did he think of his wife. He couldn't be bothered about her. She had been kidnapped. Well, people, these days, did get kidnapped. Even if he had to pay and pay, he must be rid of her.

The soft buzz of his telephone bell on his desk disrupted his thoughts.

He lifted the receiver.

'Yes?' he snapped.

'Sherry? This is Meg.' A woman's voice.

Jesus! Jamison thought. This bloody woman again!

Softening his voice, he said, 'How are you, Meg?'

'What's this about Shannon suffering from migraine? She's never had migraine before. What is this, Sherry? Shannon is the guest of honour at the Mozart recital tonight.'

'Yes, I know,' Jamison said, who didn't. 'I'm sorry, Meg. She won't be able to attend. I am worried. The doctor has given her a sedation, and right now she is asleep. She developed this blinding headache while I was in New York. The doctor assures me she will be all right in a few days.'

'Is that Doctor Macklin?'

Knowing that Macklin was Meg Clayton's doctor, he avoided the trap.

'No. I had my own specialist to take care of her. I'm sorry, Meg, but I am desperately busy. As soon as Shannon feels well enough, she will call you. My best to you and Jay,' and he hung up.

By tonight, the news that Shannon wasn't well would be all over the goddamn musical circles of the city, he thought. He had forgotten that Shannon was not only popular, but a talented cellist.

For the next quarter of an hour, his telephone rang with

people asking after Shannon. He dealt with them politely and curtly, asking them to let Shannon rest.

He kept looking at his watch. In another half hour, Kling would contact him, and he would know the conditions of the ransom. Once he knew that, he would put the plan he had in his mind into action to defeat Kling.

Getting to his feet, he walked from his study, through the big living-room and out onto the terrace to stare at the rising moon and to feel the hot breeze against his sweating face. He drew in several deep breaths, then, seeing Smyth hovering uneasily, he said, 'Get me a double Scotch and lots of ice.'

Returning to his study, he sat at his desk. He looked at the desk clock. The time now was 19.35. Soon, Kling would be telephoning him, and he would know what ransom he would be demanding.

Smyth entered and placed the Scotch that Jamison had ordered on the desk.

'You will be needing dinner, sir,' he said. 'What may I prepare for you?'

'Oh, sandwiches!' Jamison snapped. 'But later!'

'Very good, sir,' and Smyth, looking sorrowful, withdrew.

Then the telephone bell began its soft buzzing. Jamsion stiffened. Was this Kling? Or was it one of Shannon's goddamn friends? He lifted the receiver and barked, 'Yes?'

'Mr Jamison?' A man's voice.

'Yes. Who is this?'

'Chief of Police Terrell.'

Jamison felt his heart skip a beat. At some boring shindig, thrown by the Mayor, he had met Terrell and had been impressed by the man's quiet power and authority.

He forced himself to relax.

'Hello there, Terrell. Long time no see. Look, I am busy. Something I can do for you?'

'Mr Jamison, I understand that your wife was kidnapped early this morning,' Terrell said.

Blood rushed to Jamison's head. He felt a sharp pain stab him in his chest. For a long moment, he sat motionless, feeling short of breath, then he made an effort and controlled his heavy breathing.

'How do you know that?' he demanded.

'An eye-witness to the kidnapping, Mr Jamison. I am sorry about this,' Terrell said, his voice quiet. 'I want you to know we will do everything possible to be of help.'

Jamison flew into a panicky rage.

'You don't do a goddamn thing!' he shouted. 'Understand? Keep out of this. I am handling it! If you so much as fuck up this situation, I'll make you sorry! Understand?'

'I understand, Mr Jamison,' Terrell replied. 'You have the usual ransom note, saying that if you contact the police Mrs Jamison will be killed. Am I right?'

'Yes, you're right,' Jamison snarled. 'So keep out of this! When I get my wife back, you can move in, but not before!' and he slammed down the receiver.

'Very convincing, Mr Jamison,' Kling said as he appeared out of the shadows of the terrace. 'I liked that.' He moved into the light thrown by the desk lamp. 'I'm a little before my time, but I didn't want to keep you waiting.'

Jamison leaned back, glaring at Kling.

'How did the cops know we had kidnapped your wife?' Kling asked, settling himself in an armchair near Jamison's desk.

'An eye-witness,' Jamison rasped. 'And you call yourself a professional!'

Kling shrugged.

'An eye-witness or two or even three can always be fixed. Nothing to worry about, Mr Jamison. Once, when I was knocking off a fink who was causing trouble, there were five eye-witnesses.' He released a barking laugh. 'They never testified. Don't worry about eye-witnesses.'

Jamison regarded this tall, lean, grey-haired man with revulsion.

'You have gypped me, damn you!' he exclaimed.

'No . . . no. Don't get the script wrong. I had second thoughts. Now, the original plan I put before you was for me to throw a bomb that would wipe out this Irish fink, your wife, the priest and a number of oldies.' Kling shook his head. 'That's correct, isn't it? You agreed that that was the perfect way to get rid of your wife. Right?'

'It was your suggestion, and I agreed to it,' Jamison said, biting off each word. 'You now say you have had second thoughts. What thoughts?'

Kling relaxed back in his chair.

'You mightn't think it, Mr Jamison, but I am not so tough as you. I thought about knocking off thirty or so old finks just to kill your wife, and I told myself it was like killing a gnat with a sledgehammer. You get the drift of my thoughts, Mr Jamison?'

Jamison remained still and tense at his desk. He said nothing.

'The more I thought about it, the less I liked it,' Kling went on, after a pause. 'But I had agreed to do the job for you. So I thought up this kidnapping caper. It will be safe: no problems for you. I went into action and your wife is safely hidden away. As soon as you pay the ransom, her body will be found in the trunk of a stolen car. It'll be a guaranteed job. There'll be no blow-back. You will tell the cops you paid the ransom to a masked man who told you you'd find your wife in the Casino car park, safe and sound, in the trunk of a stolen car. The cops and you will find the car and find the dead body of your wife. Get the photo, Mr Jamison?' Kling lit a cigarette. 'It's a nice, safe idea. To put the icing on the cake, the ransom money will be found in the car. Two hundred thousand dollars, Mr Jamison. The cops will think it was a piker's kidnapping. The guy lost his head, killed your wife, left the ransom which might be traced and took off. Like it?'

Seething with rage, Jamison kept control of himself.

'What's the real ransom to be?' he snarled.

Kling nodded his approval.

'That's what I like about you, Mr Jamison. You get at once to the basic facts.'

'What's the ransom to be?' Jamison repeated, clenching his fists.

'You are a very rich man, Mr Jamison, and yet you are a piker. You come to me and offered me three hundred thousand to murder your wife. That was a stupid offer. Had you offered me a million, I just might have thrown a bomb. I don't say I would have, but for a million I could have been tempted. But no, you are such a piker, you offer peanuts. So, Mr Jamison, the ransom will be five million dollars to be paid into my Swiss account.'

Jamison reared back, staring at Kling.

'Five million dollars! You must be out of your mind!'

'What's five million dollars to you, Mr Jamison? That's the deal. A nice, safe, well organized job, and you'll be rid of your wife for good.'

Jamison sat still for several seconds while his mind went into action, then, satisfied with his thinking, he leaned forward, pointing his finger at Kling.

'So you think you've been smart!' he rasped. 'Now, I'll tell you something. You won't get a dollar out of me, and I'll tell you for why. In this ransom note you left, you say that unless the ransom is paid, my wife will be killed. Don't you see, you stupid hunkhead, that's what I want! I want her dead! What are you going to do with her? You'll get no money from me! So you're landed with her! Now, get out!'

Kling burst out laughing. The sound of his laughter was so genuinely amused that Jamison felt a chill run down his back. 'You heard what I said!' he shouted. 'Get out!'

'Mr Jamison, it beats me how guys like you make so much money. I guess you must be dealing with prize suckers,' Kling said. He stubbed out his cigarette. 'Tell me something, Mr Jamison, do you admire the Japanese technology?'

Jamison stared at him.

'I don't know what the hell you're talking about! I told you to get out!'

'The Japs are great people,' Kling said. 'At one time, they were imitators, but not now. They are ahead of the world in electronics. Listen to this.' He put his hand inside his jacket, then Jamison's voice came clearly into the room.

In this ransom note you left, you say that unless the ransom is paid, my wife will be killed. Don't you see, you stupid hunkhead, that's what I want.

Kling's fingers moved and the voice stopped.

'Marvellous, don't you think, Mr Jamison? Electronics. New inventions. I always carry this little gimmick around with me. When we had our interesting talk about the bomb, I had it working. I have a good tape of our conversation.'

Jamison sat motionless, stunned, then he thought of the .38 revolver he kept in his top drawer of his desk. In frustrated fury and alarm, his hand moved to the drawer.

'No, Mr Jamison. Don't try that,' Kling said gently. 'Look!'

As Jamison stared at him, an ugly-looking Beretta appeared as if by magic in Kling's hand.

'Before you even touch your gun, Mr Jamison, you're dead,' Kling said. 'Now, relax. Put your hands on your desk.' As Jamison obeyed, Kling returned the gun to its holster. 'Okay, now we can talk. You are way out of the big league, Mr Jamison. Okay, you are great when dealing with prize suckers, but not with professionals like me. Let's take a long look at the setup. I have promised to get rid of your wife. I'll do that, because in my racket when a killer fails it

127

gets known, and that's bad for my business, so I get rid of your wife. In return, you pay into my Swiss bank five million dollars. I know to a piker like, you, Mr Jamison, parting with money like that hurts. Now, if I were dealing with prize suckers as you do, I'd think this bastard was bluffing. If he gives his tapes to the cops, he would be in the same shit as I would be, so he'd be bluffing.' Kling smiled evilly. 'That would be wrong thinking, Mr Jamison. Let me spell it out. If you don't pay five million dollars into my Swiss bank, I am going to the DA and tell him a story. My story will be you hired me to murder your wife and offered to pay me three hundred thousand dollars. Now, I tell the DA that money means something to me, so I conned you. I'll tell the DA I had no intention of murdering your wife, but every intention to get your money. So the DA listens to the tapes. When he knows who you are, he will fall over himself to nail you. When you are as big as you are, you have many enemies, Mr Jamison. You have a wolf-pack behind you, waiting to pull you down. Then the press get hold of it, and they'll crucify you. Here is one of the richest men in this country, planning to get rid of his wife by murder! Man! Won't the press have a ball! So what happens? You'll be arrested and thrown into the slammer. Then, because you have lots of clout and money, you hire the best attorneys who will work like crazy to get you off the hook. But Mr Jamison, I will be willing to testify against you. When a jury hears me, you don't have a hope to beat the rap. Right. Now, first the Judge will consider me. I will have admitted to kidnapping your wife, but have returned her safe and sound. So he'll send me away for a couple of years. Then he'll take a long look at you. You will go away for at least fifteen years, Mr Jamison, and you will be ruined. Right. Now when I get sentenced, my Mafia friends will appeal and get my case – not yours – before a Mafia judge who will shake his head, fine me two thousand dollars, and I'm free again, but not you. This is the result of being a professional. Get the photo?'

For some minutes, Jamison sat still, knowing he had been completely outsmarted, then with a shrug he said, 'You don't expect me to raise five million dollars at once, do you?'

'I'll give you ten days from tomorrow,' Kling said, getting to his feet. 'If I don't hear from my Swiss bank by the eighteenth of this month, then I go visit the DA.'

'You'll get the money,' Jamison grated. 'In return, I will be rid of my wife?'

'Of course. That's no problem. Pay up, and I guarantee you'll be rid of her.'

With an airy wave of his hand, Kling walked out onto the terrace and disappeared into the darkness.

The Good Eatery restaurant offered the best value for money in the city.

With glistening eyes, Frederick Whitelaw surveyed the mountain of spaghetti, smothered in tomato and onion sauce, that had been set before him. He smiled contentedly as he fingered Chief of Police Terrell's ten-dollar bill. He had ordered chicken drumsticks in a curry sauce to follow.

As he began to attack the spaghetti, the restaurant door opened and Sydney Drysdale wandered in. He had completed his column, and had decided to have a light snack before returning home to watch a TV programme that interested him, and then go out again for his usual three course dinner.

He looked around hopefully to see if there was anyone interesting in the restaurant from whom he could get an item of news for his next day's column. He spotted Frederick Whitelaw, cramming his mouth with spaghetti.

This lad, Drysdale reminded himself, was the son of one

of the influential men in the city. Even kids get to hear things, so he waddled over to the fat boy's table.

'Hello, Freddy,' he said, pulling out a chair and sitting down. 'That looks good.'

'It is good,' the fat boy mumbled, and forked more spaghetti into his eager mouth.

'Don't you usually eat at home, Freddy?' Drysdale asked casually. 'Are you celebrating or something?'

'I sure am.' The fat boy smirked. 'The Chief of Police gave me ten bucks so I thought I'd give me a decent meal instead of the junk my mum gives me.'

Drysdale became immediately alert.

'Is that right? Now why did the Chief of Police give you ten bucks?'

'That's a secret, Mr Drysdale.' The fat boy looked sly. 'I had some information, and he parted with the money.'

'He's a nice, kind man,' Drysdale said, his smile oily. 'But ten dollars isn't a fortune. I also buy secrets, Freddy. Do you want to do a deal?'

The fat boy finished his spaghetti and sat back with a calculating expression on his face.

'That depends, Mr Drysdale,' he said after a moment of thought. 'I could sell you my secret for three hundred dollars.'

'Like father, like son,' Drydale sighed. 'This must be a big secret.'

'It sure is. It's the biggest and the most sensational secret you've ever heard.'

At this moment an elderly waitress arrived and took Drysdale's order for grilled sardines on toast. She removed the fat boy's plate and slapped down the chicken drumsticks, the curry sauce and a pile of French fried.

'You have a healthy appetite,' Drysdale said wistfully. 'It's great to be young. I'd go to one hundred bucks, but I would want to know what the secret is about.'

'Three hundred, Mr Drysdale,' the fat boy said firmly as he piled the French fried onto his plate. 'I'll tell you this. It is to do with Mr Sherman Jamison.'

Drysdale reacted as if he had been stung by a wasp.

'Mr Jamison?'

'That's right.' The fat boy cut off a bit of chicken, smothered it in curry sauce and conveyed it to his mouth. He nodded his approval. 'This is good.'

'What about Mr Jamison?' Drysdale asked, trying to sound casual.

'Well, not exactly him, but Mrs Jamison.'

'You went to the Chief of Police and told him about this, Freddy?'

'That's right. I felt I should. I was reporting a major crime.'

Drysdale began to breathe heavily.

'What major crime?'

The fat boy attacked the pile of French fried.

'It's a secret. The Chief told me to keep my mouth shut, but for three hundred dollars my mouth need not remain shut.'

Drysdale didn't hesitate. After all, this wasn't his money. His editor expected him to spend money to get news. He took out his wallet and produced three one-hundred-dollar bills which he folded.

'So, Freddy, tell me the secret.'

The fat boy eyed the money, then attacked another drumstick.

'Not until I have the money in my pocket,' he said, his mouth full. 'My old man told me always to get the money first. My old man is smart.'

'Look, Freddy, if you're conning me . . .'

'Aw, forget it! I'll tell you something, Mr Drysdale. I'm fat and look stupid, but I ain't! I could get a thousand dollars just by getting on the phone and talking to the

Washington Post, but I don't want to be bothered. Do you want to do a deal?'

Drysdale pushed the folded bills across the table. The fat boy snapped them up and stowed them away in his pocket.

'What about Mrs Jamison?' Drysdale demanded.

'Let me finish this first. My old man says it's rude to talk with one's mouth full,' the fat boy said as he began to gnaw at the chicken leg. 'This is good.'

Drysdale contained his impatience with an effort, but he felt his blood pressure rising. He sat back, trying to keep calm.

Finally the boy finished his meal and released a sigh of content.

'Man! That was good!' he exclaimed.

The waitress arrived bringing a plate containing six grilled sardines on two rounds of toast and slapped the plate before Drysdale.

'Is that all you're going to eat?' the fat boy asked.

'Never mind, Freddy, tell me the secret,' Drysdale snarled.

The fat boy leaned forward and, in a whisper, told Drysdale what he had told Chief of Police Terrell.

For a brief moment, Drysdale went into shock. *The wife of Sherman Jamison kidnapped!* This was the biggest news, the biggest scoop that had ever dropped into his lap! This kid made sense, but he must check out his story. Before going into action, he must talk to Terrell!

Shoving back his chair, Drysdale blundered to his feet. He paused only long enough to pay for his untouched meal, then scrambled into his car and headed for Police head-quarters.

The fat boy shrugged. Then he regarded the sardines. Pity to waste food, he thought. Pushing aside his empty plate, he reached forward to pick up the plate of sardines and began to eat contentedly.

This had been a rewarding evening, he thought.

Chief of Police Terrell replaced the telephone receiver and looked first at Beigler, then at Lepski. He grimaced.

'Mr Jamison confirms that his wife has been kidnapped,' he said, 'and in very forceful language told me to keep out of it. He's had the usual threat not to contact the police.'

'Did he say how much the ransom is to be?' Beigler asked.

'No. Naturally, he wants his wife back alive, and a man of his wealth wouldn't give a damn how much he has to pay.' Terrell thought for a long moment. 'Jamison carries a lot of clout. I think it would be unwise for us to start anything, but we must alert the FBI.' He looked at Beigler. 'Will you contact Howard Jackson and put him in the photo? Tell him we're doing nothing for the moment, but will want his help once Mrs Jamison is returned safely.'

Beigler nodded, got to his feet and hurried from Terrell's office to his own desk.

'Okay, Tom,' Terrell said. 'You may as well get off home. I don't think anything will develop for tonight.'

'You staying, Chief?' Lepski asked.

'I guess so.'

'Right. I'll stick around also.'

Lepski left the office and sat at his desk. He remembered Carroll. Snatching up the telephone, he asked Charlie Tanner how Carroll had reacted.

Tanner gave a whimpering moan.

'I swear to God, Tom, I'm never going to relay messages for you again! I'm still trying to recover.'

'Thanks, Charlie,' Lepski said with a crafty grin. 'You're a real pal,' and he hung up.

Ten minutes later, the telephone bell sounded on Terrell's desk.

'Charlie here, Chief,' Tanner said. 'I have Syd Drysdale asking for you.'

Terrell grimaced. He knew Drysdale only too well.

'What's he want?'

'To see you, Chief. He says it's an emergency.'

Terrell stiffened. Was it possible that Drysdale had got wind of the kidnapping?

'Okay, send him up.'

Breathing heavily, Drysdale came into Terrell's office.

'Stairs don't agree with me,' he gasped. 'I guess I eat too much.' He slumped into a chair by Terrell's desk. 'How are you, Chief? You are working late.'

Terrell regarded him, his face expressionless.

'I've got a work load. What is it, Syd?'

'I understand that Mrs Sherman Jamison was kidnapped this morning,' Drysdale said with his oily smile.

So that fat little creep had shot off his mouth! Terrell thought. He knew it would be a waste of time to fence with a man of Drysdale's experience.

'That's correct, Syd. Jamison has had a ransom note. The usual death threat if he contacts the police. He has told me in no uncertain terms to keep out of it. So I will ask you also to keep out of it.'

Drysdale nodded.

'Yeah. Jamison carries too much clout. I don't want to drop in the shit with him. When this breaks, Chief, I want your promise that I get the exclusive scoop. I also want to be kept *au fait* with how you are handling it. I take it Jackson of the FBI will be brought into this when Mrs Jamison is returned.'

'Of course. Now, Syd, I can't make any promises,' Terrell said. 'As soon as the news breaks, the press of the world will jump on the band-wagon.'

Drysdale scratched his fat nose.

'I'll give you a *quid pro quo*. You hold off the wolf-pack until I file my story, and I'll give you a lead to who the kidnapper is.'

Terrell stared at him.

'You know who the kidnapper is?'

'I don't *know*, but I can make a very close and sound guess. I just want your promise to get me the exclusive. After all, what have you got to work on? Suppose Jamison pays the ransom? Suppose he gets his wife back? The kidnapper will vanish. You have no lead to him, but I am pretty sure I have.'

Terrell hesitated. No threats of withholding evidence would bother Drysdale.

'Okay, Syd, you get your exclusive. Who do you think pulled the kidnapping?'

'Word of honour?' Drysdale asked, his little eyes probing.

'You'll get your exclusive. Now tell me!'

Drydale beamed. He leaned forward and said quietly, 'I'm willing to bet my Sunday lunch that the man who fixed the kidnapping is Lucky Lucan.'

8

Kling strode into his cabin at the Star Motel, slamming and locking the door behind him.

He found Ng Vee standing by the kitchen stove, stirring a saucepan of savoury-smelling food.

'That smells great,' Kling said. 'I'm starving! What is it?'

'Curried beef, rice and green peppers, sir,' Ng said, not looking at Kling. 'It'll be ready in five minutes.'

'Great!' Kling moved out of the kitchen. 'We'll talk as we eat.'

He turned on the TV set. He was feeling triumphant. In ten days' time, he would be worth five million dollars! He had certainly handled this sonofabitch Jamison beautifully. He stared for a moment at a busty girl screaming into a mike and, grimacing, he switched off the set.

The table was laid. He nodded. This kid certainly was a find! He never seemed to put a foot wrong, and his cooking was out of this world.

Kling took his place at the table and began to nibble bread.

Five million dollars!

He would be able to kiss the Mafia bosses goodbye. He would no longer have to plan to knock off some pest. With five million dollars, he would be able to live as he had so often dreamed of living.

Ng came in and set a big dish of the curried beef and a side plate of fried bananas and rice before Kling.

'Terrific, kid!' Kling said, as he began to pile the food on his plate. 'Man! I'm starving!'

He didn't notice that Ng only helped himself to a token

portion of the food. Nor did he notice that Ng only toyed with his food while he ate ferociously.

After ten minutes or so, Kling, his hunger slightly appeased, grinned at Ng.

'How did it go, kid? How did she behave?'

His face expressionless, Ng said, 'No problem, sir.'

Kling gave his short, barking laugh.

'Come the day, kid, when you say there *is* a problem. Then I'll really get worried.' He shovelled more food into his mouth. 'This is top-class,' he went on. 'What happened when she surfaced?'

Ng moved his food around with his fork.

'She was very calm, sir,' he said. 'I explained that she had been kidnapped. There was no trouble. She accepted the situation.'

Kling continued to eat.

'You've done a great job, kid. Now, I'll tell you something. I've talked to Jamison. In ten days, he's going to part with five million dollars. I had him in a squeeze. There was nothing else he could do. So, in ten days' time, I'll be worth five million dollars! And, as you're always saying, with no problems. How do you like that, kid?'

'I am glad for you, sir,' Ng said. He felt if he put any more food in his mouth, he would throw up. 'What will happen to Mrs Jamison?'

'I'll tell you what I'm going to do when I get this money,' Kling said, ignoring Ng's question. 'I'm going to charter a big yacht, and I'm going to drift around the world.' Kling's smile widened. 'I want you to come with me. Get it?'

Ng bowed politely.

'Thank you, sir.' He got to his feet and began to gather up the dishes. 'I have an ice with fruit, sir, if you would like it.'

Kling shoved back his chair and stood up.

'No. I've had enough. A great meal, kid. You know what

I'm going to do now? I'm going to town to celebrate earning five million bucks! I'm going to find a red head, well stuffed into her dress, and I'm going to screw her until she yells blue murder!'

Ng continued to collect the dishes.

'Yes, sir,' he said.

'Hey, kid! Let's go together. It's time you had a girl,' Kling said. 'Come on! Leave that junk. Let's you and me paint the town red.'

'Thank you, sir, but please excuse me. I would rather watch TV if you don't mind.'

'Jesus!' Kling exclaimed. 'What a character you are!'

'Yes, sir. May I ask what will happen to Mrs Jamison?'

As Kling lit a cigarette, his face turned ruthless.

'What do you think, kid? Let me spell it out. I am a professional killer. When someone comes to me and tells me he wants someone rubbed out because he or she is a nuisance, and if this guy gives me the money I ask for, then I do the job. I've worked for years with the Mafia. They know I can be relied on. They don't give a damn if I do an occasional private job, but they would give a damn if the word got out that I hadn't delivered. So, you ask what will happen to this woman? So, I'll tell you. She's going to be rubbed out, and you and I will go on a world cruise.'

Holding the dishes, Ng stood motionless, looking like an ivory statue.

He asked, in a low, flat voice, 'How will you kill her, sir?'

Kling shrugged impatiently.

'I have ten days to think about that . . . nothing messy.' He looked thoughtfully at Ng. 'Suppose you do your blood-vessel trick? How about it, kid?'

Ng shivered.

'I have never killed a woman, sir.'

Kling grinned.

'There's always a first time. Think about it,' and with a

wave of his hand he unlocked the cabin door and went out into the hot, humid darkness to his car.

Half an hour later, the dishes washed and put away and the kitchen once more spick and span, Ng walked into the living-room and sat down.

She is going to be rubbed out.

Kling's words burned in Ng's brain.

He sat huddled up, his clenched fists gripped between his knees, and he kept thinking of those words. A sick horror engulfed him. This lovely, gentle woman would be ruthlessly killed. He thought of Kling: a man who had saved him from starvation and raised his mother from utter poverty, who had taken care of him and had treated him as a loyal partner.

A little moan of agony escaped from Ng's tightly closed lips.

How could he save the life of this lovely woman without being disloyal to his master? After what Kling had done for him and his mother, it would be unthinkable for him to be disloyal!

Ten days!

At least there was time to think and perhaps plan. Ng forced himself to relax. Surely in ten days, some solution would arrive.

Sitting back in the big lounging-chair, his mind shifted to those two wonderful hours he had spent with Shannon Jamison.

The memory was so vivid, it was as if he were watching a movie.

Again, he saw her, lying, unconscious on the bed. He had waited, then finally he saw her stir, then slowly open her eyes. He watched her puzzled expression as she looked up at the quilted, white ceiling. Then she lifted her head and looked directly at him.

139

He smiled at her, willing kindness and love into his smile.

He saw her stiffen, close her eyes as if absorbing a shock, then those beautiful eyes opened, and she half sat up.

'It's all right, ma'am,' he said softly. 'You have nothing to fear.'

Shannon stared at this slightly built Vietnamese. She felt she was dreaming.

'Who are you?' she forced herself to ask.

'It it all right, ma'am. Please don't be alarmed.'

She looked hurriedly around the big, well furnished room without windows, then back to him.

'Where am I? What's happening?'

'Ma'am, you have been kidnapped. I am here to look after you. Please, you have nothing to worry about.'

'Kidnapped?'

Shannon swung her long legs off the bed and sat up. She possessed considerable strength of character. She refused to let herself panic and forced herself to remain calm.

'Are you telling me that I have been kidnapped?'

Ng nodded.

'Yes, ma'am.'

She looked around the room.

'Where am I?'

'I'm sorry, ma'am. I can't tell you that.'

She took a long steady look at Ng. She saw he was a Vietnamese, and she was quick to see he was regarding her the way a spaniel dog regards his mistress. This expression gave her confidence.

'Who are you?' she asked.

Ng hesitated, then said, 'Call me Kim, ma'am. Would you like coffee? You have only to ask and I will do anything to please you.'

She felt this odd-looking youth was on her side, so she forced a smile.

'Thank you, Kim. Yes, I would like a cup of coffee.'

Ng moved swiftly into the kitchen and heated up the prepared coffee while Shannon got to her feet, found the bathroom and shut herself in. Her toilet finished, she returned to the bedroom.

Kidnapped!

This must mean that Sherman would have to pay ransom, then she would be free again. Then a thought struck her.

Would Sherman pay the ransom?

For a long time now, she had had this feeling that her husband wanted to get rid of her. If she died, he would be free to marry this woman she knew existed. No! she told herself. Sherman couldn't be so ruthless as that! He would pay the ransom. Very soon the press would know she had been kidnapped. There would be a tremendous outcry. Surely, Sherman wouldn't dare not pay the ransom!

Ng came in, carrying a tray.

'If you would like something to eat, ma'am, I can easily prepare you something.'

'Thank you. Just coffee.' She forced herself to smile at him and waited while he poured the coffee and gave her a cup.

'Thank you.' She sipped the coffee, then regarded him. 'You make excellent coffee, Kim.'

Ng was overwhelmed. How he loved this beautiful, gracious woman!

'Thank you, ma'am.' He hesitated, then went on, 'I am afraid you will have to stay here for a few days. Is there anything I can get you? Please ask.'

Shannon finished her coffee while her mind raced. She must know more details of this kidnapping.

'Does my husband know I have been kidnapped?' she asked as Ng refilled her cup.

'Oh, yes, ma'am. He knows.'

'That tall thin man who talked to me before I blacked out,' Shannon said. 'He is the kidnapper . . . not you?'

141

Ng hesitated.

'That's right, ma'am.'

'And you do what he tells you?'

Again Ng hesitated. He was becoming uneasy at these questions, but he wanted her to regard him as her friend.

'Yes, ma'am,' he said finally. 'I'm sorry, but there is nothing more I can tell you. Is there something I can get for you? The refrigerator has lots of food, but there may be something else you need.'

'I'm to stay here for several days?'

'I'm afraid so, ma'am.'

'Kim, I don't know if my husband will pay the ransom. What will happen to me if he doesn't pay?'

She saw Ng flinch and his hands turn into fists.

'He will pay, ma'am,' Ng said earnestly. 'My master has told me so.'

'How can you be so sure, Kim?'

'He *has* to pay, ma'am. My master has told me so.'

'Your master?' Shannon drank more coffee. 'How odd for you to call a kidnapper your master.'

Ng had a sudden feeling he was talking too much. He wanted to talk. He wanted to tell this lovely woman how much he loved her. He wanted to tell her about his past life, but he restrained himself.

'Is there anything I can get for you, ma'am?'

Shannon realized that he had gone on the defensive, and for the moment she had lost him. She knew she would get nothing further from him, but she also felt, if she handled him gently, he would co-operate.

'Yes, please, Kim. If I have to stay here for some days, I would like a radio. Could you get that for me?'

'Oh, yes, ma'am,' Ng said eagerly. 'That's no problem.'

'Then the other thing I would like is a Bible.'

She saw Ng stiffen, then he stared at her.

'A Bible?'

142

'I think you are a good Catholic as I am,' Shannon said, quick to see his reaction. 'Yes, please . . . a Bible.'

Ng's mind flashed back to the priest who had taught him English and how to write, his kindness, his understanding and his religious instruction.

'Yes, ma'am. I'll be back soon.'

The film going on in Ng's mind faded.

He had bought a small transistor and a Bible out of the housekeeping money that Kling had given him. He had returned to the Whipping room and was glad and sorry that Shannon was in the bathroom. He paused, listening to the sound of water filling the bath, then he placed the radio and the Bible on the occasional table, paused for a long moment to stare wistfully at the bathroom door, then went out into the lonely sunshine.

Looking around at Beigler, Lepski and Howard Jackson, Terrell said, 'Drysdale has fingered Lucky Lucan for the kidnapping.'

'That I can't believe!' Lepski said with a snort. 'That wet creep wouldn't have the guts to kidnap a mouse!'

'You're right, Tom,' Terrell said, 'but it looks as if he just might have steered the kidnappers to Mrs Jamison. Drysdale said Lucan came to him for information about Jamison and his wife. Then this morning, Drysdale saw Lucan talking to a tough-looking, thin man who could match the boy's description. When Drysdale questioned Lucan about Mrs Jamison, Lucan seemed to fall apart and got in a panic. That's all we have to go on, but it makes a picture.'

'The tough-looking man?' Jackson asked.

'Lucan says he's just a neighbour and doesn't know his name, according to Drysdale. It would be helpful to find out if this tough-looking man has a companion.'

'That's easy,' Jackson said. 'The Star Motel? So suppose

I put one of my women operators there. She can rent a cabin and watch.'

'That's a good thought,' Terrell said, nodding. 'We have to tread carefully, Jackson. Neither Lucan nor this tough must get the idea we are checking them out.'

'Leave it to me, Chief. I've just the womam,' Jackson said. 'I'll get her there in a couple of hours,' and he reached for the telephone.

Lucan was in a state of near panic. If Kling hadn't promised to pay him half a million dollars, he would have packed and fled back to New York, but he was sure Kling would never part with the money unless he stayed.

Drysdale's unexpected visit had almost destroyed Lucan's nerves.

As Lucan paced up and down in the living-room of his cabin, he kept asking himself if Drysdale knew that the Jamison woman had been kidnapped. Was Drysdale sniffing for a clue or was he just trying to satisfy his curiosity?

Lucan cursed himself for losing his nerve and had reacted so stupidly when Drysdale had asked him how he had got on with the Jamisons. That could have been a harmless question, but Lucan now was sure that by his stupid reaction he had aroused Drysdale's insatiable curiosity.

Hearing a car start up, he hurried to the window in time to see Kling drive away.

He looked at his watch. The time was 20.40. He realized he had been pacing the floor for the best part of two hours, worrying and sweating. He felt mildly hungry. He decided to drive down to the city and have dinner at one of the many sea-food restaurants. Maybe he could find a woman who would help him pass the night. If he didn't relax, he told himself, he would go out of his skull.

He took a quick shower, put on a fresh shirt, then, turning off the lights, he went out into the steamy darkness.

As he was locking the door, a small car pulled up.

'Excuse me.' A girl's voice. 'Can you tell me which is cabin twenty-four?'

Turning, Lucan surveyed the girl who had just got out of the car. She stood in the hard light from the roof of the motel and smiled at him.

Lucan felt his blood quicken. Some chick! he thought.

She was tall, slim, wearing skin-tight jeans and a T-shirt. What this get-up did to her figure startled Lucan. Some body! he thought. She was pretty in a sophisticated way: blonde curls, big blue eyes and a wide, sensual mouth.

'Cabin 24?' he said, turning on his charming smile. 'Right next door. I'm Julian Lucan. Looks like I'm going to be your neighbour. Are you here for long?'

'I'm Beryl Shaddock. Call me Berry,' the girl said. 'Sure, I'm staying for at least a week. I'm waiting for my husband to join me.' She pouted. 'He's always joining me some place or the other.'

Lucan smiled again. He liked nothing better than pretty wives whose husbands were joining them sooner or later.

'Anything I can do to help, Berry?'

'Well, I've got a suitcase.' She looked helpless. 'Perhaps . . . ?' She flicked open the trunk of the car.

'Sure.' Lucan heaved out the heavy bag. 'Give me the key. I'll see you settled.'

Together they entered the cabin. Lucan switched on the lights and placed the bag by the bed.

'That's real nice of you, Julian,' the girl said. 'Well, thanks a million.'

'Maybe we'll be seeing each other,' Lucan said as he moved to the door. 'I know this city. I could show you around.'

'You could?' Her smile brightened. 'I'd love that.'

'Okay,' Lucan said. He was getting the idea that this well built chick could be a push-over.

145

'I'm starving,' she said, thrusting her breasts at him. 'I've flown from New York and the food on the plane was just terrible. Can I eat here?'

'Sure, but the food here is also terrible,' Lucan said, seeing his chance. 'I'm just going to a little sea-food restaurant. Be my guest.'

'Could I? Marvellous!' Her blue eyes flashed. 'You are so kind, Julian!'

'Fine. Come as you are. You look terrific. Knock on my cabin door when you're fixed.'

Of course, Lucan wasn't to know that Beryl Shaddock was an FBI agent, Howard Jackson's plant. Nor, of course, would he know that this seemingly sexy-looking girl was one of the best FBI agents in Florida: that she was an expert karate fighter, an expert pistol shot and tougher than teak.

As soon as Lucan had returned to his cabin, Beryl ran into the bathroom, washed, fixed her face, then ran to her suitcase. From it she extracted a two-way radio. In moments, she was speaking softly to Jackson, with Lepski, who had been given the task to work with Jackson, listening in.

'Going like a dream,' she whispered. 'I'm having dinner with Lucan right now.'

Jackson chortled.

'Marvellous girl! Now look, take it slow. Lucan is no fool. Give him a good time. Just get him to relax. I want to know about the tough character he was talking to. Get it?'

'I'm with you. Over and out.'

Beryl replaced the two-way radio and locked the bag. Then, leaving her cabin, being careful to lock the door, she moved along the sandy path and knocked on Lucan's door.

Half an hour later, Lucan was seated at a table for two in one of the better sea-food restaurants, facing Beryl.

'Hmmm!' she said. 'I'm starving to death.'

'Let me choose for you,' Lucan said.

The Maître d' appeared and Lucan ordered dressed crabs, followed by a dish of clams, big prawns, corn on the cob, boiled potatoes and a lobster each.

While waiting, Beryl chatted. She was an expert at saying nothing, but holding a man's interest. She kept leaning forward so Lucan could get a good look at her cleavage. She told him her husband (she wasn't married) was in real estate and was setting up in Miami. Lucan, scarcely listening, kept staring at her half-concealed breasts. It wasn't until they had eaten the crab and were drinking white wine that Beryl said casually, 'Tell me about my neighbours, Julian. Are there any as handsome as you?'

Her sexy blue eyes were watching him, and she saw him stiffen.

'Just a bunch of old squares,' he said curtly. 'You don't have to bother your pretty head about them.'

She laughed.

'Why should I? Tell me about Paradise City.'

On safe ground, Lucan relaxed again. He was an amusing talker and while they ate the main course he kept her laughing. All the time, he was wondering if he could get her into his bed. She seemed easy, but he was so experienced with women, he knew he had to approach cautiously.

The meal over, Lucan suggested they went on to the Casino and dance.

'Julian, please excuse me,' Beryl said, caressing his arm. 'I'm terribly tired.' She leaned forward and brushed his cheek with her lips. 'Could we make it tomorrow?'

Lucan didn't know whether to be disappointed or excited.

'Okay, babe,' he said. 'I understand. You really mean we have a date for tomorrow night?'

She gave a sexy little moan.

'Oh, yes, you handsome, marvellous man!' She had to control herself not to burst out laughing at this corny dialogue.

147

'I'll see you home,' Lucan said.

'Oh no! You find a nice girl – not as nice as I am – but find her, and we'll really get together tomorrow night. I'll take a taxi.'

Now, completely hooked, Lucan put his arm around her, fondling her breasts, and moved with her to his car.

'You go back with me, baby,' he said. 'I'll take a sleeping pill and dream of tomorrow night.'

Sitting beside him, as he drove back to the motel, in the darkness, Beryl frowned.

Not a profitable evening information-wise, she thought, but at least she had had an excellent dinner at Lucan's expense. Howard had warned her to take it slow. So, okay, tomorrow was another day.

But action for her started as Lucan pulled up outside her cabin.

Standing unsteadily in the glare of the roof lights, a half bottle of Scotch in his hand was Kling.

Kling had gone to the Casino, looking for a girl, but not finding one who suited him, he got good and drunk. He had been gently eased out of the Casino and into his car. The guards of the Casino had a lot of experience handling drunks. Kling let them put him in his car and start the car engine.

He had no idea how he had reached the Star Motel. His one thought now was to lie on his bed and drink more Scotch.

'Oh, God!' Lucan exclaimed when he saw Kling staggering towards him. 'This could mean trouble, Berry.'

'Who's this?' she asked.

'A goddamn drunk who lives in a cabin not far from me,' Lucan said, hurriedly getting out of his car. 'You sit still, babe. I'll handle him.'

As Kling weaved towards them, Beryl saw he was tall, thin and tough-looking. She gave Lucan a moment, then got out of the car.

By then Kling had arrived.

'Hi, Lucky!' he bawled. 'Any chick? I went to town and, goddamn it, couldn't find a screw.'

'Shut up!' Lucan snapped. 'You're drunk!'

'Sure, I'm drunk,' Kling bawled, then he saw Beryl as she stood by the car. 'Hey! Hey! What have you got there?'

'Get the hell out!' Lucan snapped. 'Come on, Ernie, you're making a goddamn exhibition of yourself.'

'You are certainly lucky, Lucky,' Kling said and leered at Beryl. 'Hi, baby! If you feel like changing partners, I'm in the market.'

Then Ng appeared into the glaring light. He took hold of Kling by his wrist and pulled him back. Kling stumbled, and hung onto Ng, mumbling, then Ng guided him down the sandy path and into their cabin. The door shut.

'Well . . .' Beryl laughed. 'High life at the Star Motel. Who was that?'

'I told you,' Lucan said, sweating. 'Just a goddamn drunk. I'm sorry about this.'

'Why did he call you Lucky?'

'Forget it. He's a drunk.'

'And that odd-looking boy. He looked Vietnamese to me. Who is he?'

'God knows.' Lucan was getting into a panic. 'His servant, I guess. I tell your baby, I'm sorry about this.'

She patted his arm.

'I thought it was fun. Then see you tomorrow.' She gave him a quick kiss on his cheek, then, unlocking the door of her cabin, turning to give him a wave, she entered and closed the door.

Three minutes later she was talking to Howard Jackson on her two-way radio.

The time was ten minutes after midnight.

Terrell sat at his desk, facing Howard Jackson and Lepski as he listened to Jackson's report.

'Looks like we have a big lead,' Jackson said. 'My operator has done a great job in a short time. She's got in real with Lucan. Returning to the motel, they encountered a drunk who called Lucan "Lucky". This is the tall thin, tough-looking guy that Drysdale tipped.' He went on to describe what had happened outside the motel. 'Now, this is interesting. A young slim Vietnamese man took the drunk away. These two seem to match the description of the two men who kidnapped Mrs Jamison by the kid. My operator is going to check them out. By tomorrow, we'll have their names. Maybe they will have records. My operator might be able to get into their cabin and lift some fingerprints. She's good at that.'

Terrell shook his head.

'No! We wait until Jamison gives us the green light that he has paid the ransom and got Mrs Jamison back. Tell your operator to lay off. This is too dangerous. If we make one slip, Mrs Jamison could be murdered, and then Jamison will really start big trouble.'

Jackson grimaced, then shrugged.

'Okay. This is your neck of the woods. But when the ransom is paid, we move in fast?'

Terrell nodded.

'Yes, but not before Mrs Jamison is returned.'

As Beryl was relaxing in her bed, ready to sleep, her two-way radio, lying on her pillow, came alive.

'Beryl?'

'Right here.' Her mind became alert.

'The orders are to play this one cool. Do nothing further. The cops are shit-scared of Jamison. So, just enjoy yourself, keep your eyes open, but no action until I give you the green light . . . understand?'

'That's great news!' Beryl said sarcastically. 'Now, listen

to me! I've got involved with Lucan. He expects to drag me into his bed tomorrow night. I think he is an utter creep and the last man I'd want to bed with. I need help, Howard. I want my supposed husband to arrive pronto tomorrow morning. If he doesn't, I'm packing and leaving!'

Jackson sighed.

'Okay. I'll be there. Maybe it's a good idea. I'll be able to take a look at these two guys.'

'That's what I thought. And listen, Howard, there are two beds in this cabin. No funny business! I'm not all that mad about you either.'

'Beryl! I'm shocked. I am a respectably married man!'

'I know. I've already met too many respectably married men. They *are* married, but there's nothing respectable about them! No funny business!' And Beryl switched off.

Lepski arrived home at 01.15. He was in no mood to put up with Carroll's tantrums. There were times – not many – when he asserted himself.

He was tired, and there was some thought that kept nagging at the back of his mind which he couldn't pin down. This infuriated him and turned him sour.

He found Carroll sitting before the TV, absorbed in a soap opera. She didn't look at him as he came into the living-room.

'Don't speak to me!' she snapped. 'I've almost had enough of you, Lepski! A movie and a dinner! That's a big laugh!'

Lepski strode to the TV set and snapped it off just when the doe-eyed heroine seemed about to be raped.

With a scream of rage Carroll jumped to her feet.

'Shut up!' Lepski snarled in his cop voice. 'Listen! We've got the biggest case we've ever had! Sherman Jamison's wife has been kidnapped!'

Carroll's rage evaporated as she stared at her husband.

151

'Mrs Jamison . . . kidnapped!'

'Correct. A real big deal! The Chief is scared that Jamison will make trouble, so all this is strictly under the rug until the ransom has been paid and Mrs Jamison returned. The FBI have moved in, and I'm working with them. I've got to get some sleep. Tomorrow will be one hell of a day!'

'Oh, Tom. I wasn't to know.' Carroll came to him and put her arms around him. 'Come on! We'll go to bed.'

In spite of Carroll's ministrations, Lepski spent a restless night. There was this thought that kept nagging at him, far back in his subconscious. He came awake at 07.30 and the nagging thought suddenly jelled. Clearly into his mind came the memory of Lucky Lucan leaving Lucy Loveheart's brothel.

He recalled how puzzled he had been that a gigolo like Lucan should be calling on Lucy Loveheart. He stiffened. Lucan had been fingered by Drysdale as a possible go-between for the kidnappers. Suppose the kidnappers had asked Lucan to find a safe-house in which to hide Mrs Jamison? What could be safer than Lucy Loveheart's brothel? A hunch? Well, hunches were all part of police business.

Galvanized, Lepski sprang out of bed and rushed into the bathroom where he showered and shaved hastily. As he returned to the bedroom he heard Carroll was already in the kitchen. He threw on his clothes to the smell of grilling ham.

'Have you thought of something, Tom?' Carroll asked as he stormed into the living-room.

'Yes! I've got to get moving fast!'

'You'll eat your breakfast first,' Carroll said firmly. She placed a plate of four fried eggs and grilled ham before him as he sat down.

'A cop's real wife!' Lepski said and grinned at her as he attacked the food.

'What have you thought?' Carroll asked, sitting at the table.

'Never mind,' Lepski mumbled, his mouth full. 'It's a hunch. I think I know where they could be hiding Mrs Jamison.'

'Careful you don't choke yourself,' Carroll said anxiously as she watched Lepski bolting down the food. She poured coffee. 'Where do you think they've hidden her?'

'It'd take too long to tell you,' Lepski said, then drank the coffee, shoved aside his plate and jumped to his feet. 'See you, honey,' and, grabbing his hat, he rushed out to his car.

While Lepski was bolting down his breakfast, Kling came awake from a sodden sleep with a king-sized hangover. He felt as if someone was slamming a sledgehammer inside his skull. He groaned, holding his head. Slowly, he peeled open his eyes to find Ng standing over him.

'Perhaps coffee, sir?' Ng asked.

Kling snarled at him. When suffering from a hangover, he was at his vicious worst.

'Nothing! Get the hell out!'

'Sir. May I take the car?' Ng asked.

'Take any goddamn thing! Get the hell out!'

All night, after getting Kling into bed, Ng had thought of Shannon Jamison. This beautiful, gentle woman must not die, Ng kept telling himself as he tossed and turned in his bed. But how to save her without being disloyal to his master? His mind had shifted to Kling. This man had done so much for him and his mother. Ng moaned softly to himself. He was sure that Kling would kill this woman as he would kill a fly. How to save her?

There was time . . . ten days. Ng thought of the pleasure he would get, seeing Shannon again. He would get her flowers and breakfast.

Watched by Beryl from her window, he got in the car and

153

drove down to the highway. While Kling had been snoring in his bed, Ng had taken a fifty-dollar bill from Kling's well stuffed wallet. The only place where Ng could buy flowers was at the airport. He bought roses and two orchids. By the time he reached Lucy Loveheart's residence, Lepski was parked opposite, waiting and hopefully watching.

He saw Ng drive down into the garage.

A slimly built Vietnamese!

Lepski slid out of his car. He was elated. It looked as if his hunch was paying off! Cautiously, he walked down the ramp of the underground garage in time to see the elevator's indicator show that the cage had gone to the top floor.

Returning to his car, he now felt almost certain that Sherman Jamison's wife was hidden on the top floor of Lucy Loveheart's brothel.

With the patience of a dedicated cop, Lepski lit a cigarette, settled himself and awaited further developments.

Unaware that he had been watched, Ng stood before the door of the Whipping room, his heart thumping. He clutched the bouquet of flowers. He tapped on the door. When he heard nothing, he tapped again.

Shannon who had passed a restless night, hearing the persistent tapping, started up from the bed. With a clutch of fear, she called, 'Who is it?'

'It's Kim, ma'am,' Ng said. 'May I come in?'

Shannon gave a gasp of relief. She felt she could handle this odd Vietnamese.

'Yes, come in. Give me five minutes.' She slid out of the bed and went into the bathroom.

'I'm sorry to be so early, ma'am,' Ng said as he entered the living-room. 'I wanted to give you breakfast.'

Shannon didn't hear any of this as she was in the bathroom.

154

Finding a vase, Ng filled it with water and arranged the flowers. He set the vase on the table, then went into the kitchen and made coffee.

He was setting the table as Shannon came in. She was wearing a kimono that Lucan had bought and, to Ng, she looked so beautiful he caught his breath.

'Ma'am, some toast?' he asked, regarding her with adoring eyes.

'No, thank you. Coffee will be fine,' Shannon said, then, seeing the flowers, she exclaimed, 'How lovely! Thank you, Kim. How kind you are!'

'It is nothing, ma'am.' He poured the coffee. 'I do hope you found the food acceptable. I have been worrying. These frozen packs aren't much.' He held a chair for her to sit down at the table. 'I would so much like to cook you a good lunch. Would you allow me to do this, please? I can prepare you an excellent meal of saffron rice chicken with lychee. Would you like that, ma'am?'

Shannon stirred sugar into her coffee, her mind active. She had now come to the conclusion that this odd Vietnamese youth had fallen in love with her.

'That sounds marvellous, Kim.' She forced a smile. 'I'd love that.'

'I will arrange it, ma'am. It will give me great pleasure.'

She sipped the excellent coffee and regarded him.

'Kim, please be frank with me. I feel you are a friend. I am a prisoner here, and I do realize how fortunate I am to have such a nice, kind jailer. I am worried. My husband and I don't get along any more.' She put down the cup. 'He wants to marry another woman. I keep asking myself if he will pay the ransom for me to be released.'

Ng nodded.

'Oh, yes, ma'am. I've already told you. He will have to pay the ransom. My master has him in a squeeze. You have nothing to worry about.'

'What squeeze?' Shannon asked, forcing her voice to sound casual.

'That I can't tell you, ma'am. I promise you, when the ransom is paid, you will be safe.'

'There is another thing that worries me,' Shannon said, looking directly at Ng. 'A few months ago, my husband suffered a heart attack. Suppose he had a fatal attack before the ransom was paid. What would happen to me?'

Ng stared at her.

'Whatever happens, you will go free.' He moved to the door. 'I will arrange your lunch. You have nothing to worry about.'

As he rode down in the elevator, his mind churned with excitement.

Here was the solution!

With Jamison dead, there would be no ransom. This lovely woman would be freed. His master would lose interest. No money . . . no killing.

He felt confident he could get into Jamison's villa and kill him.

That was the solution!

There was time. First, he wanted to show this lovely woman how well he could cook. As he walked up the ramp of the garage, he reminded himself of the ingredients he would have to buy.

As he hurried along the sidewalk towards the big self-service store, Lepski slid out of his car and followed him.

9

Jamison's executive jet touched down at the Zurich airport at 09.30.

The previous afternoon he had told Smyth to alert his pilot to be ready to take off for Switzerland, and for Smyth to book a suite at the *Baur au Lac* hotel, and to alert Maurice Felder, the President of the Swiss branch of the Jamison Computer Organization, that he wished to see him, immediately he arrived.

Jamison was met by one of the senior executives who carried his bag, saw him through the douane and to the Rolls Royce that the hotel used to meet VIP clients.

He was received at the hotel with obsequious bows and conducted to a suite overlooking the lake. Having shaved, showered and changed, Jamsion went down to the hotel entrance where the Rolls drove him to the sumptuous offices of the Corporation.

Maurice Felder, the President, received him with a warm handshake.

'Most unexpected, Mr Jamison,' he said as Jamison sat down. 'A very pleasant, and gratifying surprise.'

Felder was a tall bulky man in his late fifties, always immaculately dressed, balding and, as Jamison knew, one of the shrewdest and most knowledgeable Swiss in the country. What Felder didn't know about big business, industry, banking and big money wasn't worth knowing.

'I have a personal problem,' Jamison said abruptly. 'I want to know everything there is to know about Banque Bovay. What can you tell me?'

As Felder sat behind his desk, he lifted his bushy eyebrows.

'A small, private bank. There are, of course, a number of these in Zurich, Bern, Basle and Geneva. These small banks give individual service, don't ask awkward questions and extend the recognized banking secrecy to foreigners. This particular bank has been in the hands of the Bovay family for the past fifty years. Henri Bovay who had been running the bank for the past twenty years has just retired. His son, Paul, has taken his place. I understand that Henri Bovay suffered a stroke, and now has nothing to do with the bank. Paul Bovay seems to be doing a good job. The bank, in a small way, is prosperous. Its assets are acceptable.' Felder paused and regarded Jamison. 'Is this the kind of information you need, Mr Jamison?'

'When did the son take over the bank?'

'Only last month.'

'Tell me more about the father.'

Felder, aware that he had an important board meeting in twenty minutes' time, smiled his humourless Swiss smile.

'Perhaps you would be good enough first to tell me what the problem is, Mr Jamison, and why you are interested in a small concern like the Bovay Bank. I could then give you direct information without wasting your time.'

'Or wasting your time,' Jamison said with a nod of approval. All his dealings with Felder had been excellent. Felder was one of the few men that Jamison considered a top-class executive.

Felder lifted his fat hands.

'Yes, Mr Jamison. I have a board meeting.'

'Right. Here's the problem. My wife has been kidnapped.'

Felder stiffened.

'I am sorry to hear this, Mr Jamison. So . . . ?'

158

'The ransom of five million dollars is to be paid to the Bovay Bank. The kidnapper whose name is Ernie Kling has an account at this bank. Kling is an American citizen. Unless the ransom is paid, he tells me he will murder my wife. He has given me his account number at the Bovay Bank. I need to prove to him that this sum has been paid into his account before my wife is set free.'

Felder sat for a long moment, pulling at his underlip, then he picked up the telephone receiver that connected him with his secretary.

'The board meeting is to be cancelled,' he said. 'I don't wish to be disturbed,' and he hung up. 'Yes, Mr Jamison, this is a problem.' He looked directly at Jamison. 'Tell me your thinking.'

'I want my wife free,' Jamison lied.

Felder nodded._

'Of course.'

'But I'm damned if I'm going to pay this kidnapper five million dollars,' Jamison went on.

Felder again nodded.

'There is always a solution to any problem. May I ask you to leave this with me? I believe you are staying at the *Baur au Lac*?'

'Yes.'

'I suggest we meet there for dinner tonight,' Felder said. 'Would eight o'clock be convenient?'

'Yes.'

'You have this man Kling's account number at the Bovay Bank?'

'I have it.' Jamison took from his wallet the scrap of paper Kling had given him. It was in a plastic envelope. He passed the envelope to Felder who wrote down the number, then returned the envelope to Jamison.

'By this evening, I hope to have found a satisfactory solution.' Felder got to his feet. 'Please be patient, Mr

Jamison, this isn't going to be easy, and I will need a little time.'

'I understand. Thank you, Felder.' Jamison got to his feet. 'I have every confidence in you.' Then, lying, Jamison went on, 'I don't have to tell you that my wife's life must not be at risk.'

'That, of course, is understood. As you are here, would you care to inspect the factory? I can arrange a conducted tour.'

'No!' Jamison barked. 'I'm not in the mood. Then at eight o'clock tonight.' Shaking hands, he left.

Felder sat at his desk and snatched up the telephone receiver.

'Get me Mr Paul Bovay of the Bovay Bank,' he told his secretary.

Lepski burst into Chief of Police Terrell's office and slid to a standstill.

'Chief! I've found her!' he bawled.

Terrell, with a mass of papers on his desk, looked up with barely suppressed impatience and regarded Lepski. 'Found who?' he asked.

'Mrs Jamison! Who else?'

Terrell pushed back his chair.

'You have found Mrs Jamison?'

'I got a hunch,' Lepski said, loosening his tie. 'I'm willing to bet she's stashed away in Lucy Loveheart's whore-house!'

Terrell rubbed his nose.

'Sit down, Tom. Take it easy,' he said. 'Tell me.'

Briefly, Lepski made his report. How he had seen Lucan leave the brothel, how he had this hunch, how he had sat outside the brothel and seen the slim Vietnamese drive down to the garage, how he had seen the elevator go to the top floor.

'This Viet left about an hour later and went marketing. I followed him,' Lepski went on. 'He bought a chicken and various herbs and a pack of rice, then he returned to the whore-house. So it's my bet that Mrs Jamison is there.'

'You don't *know* she's there. Okay, it looks good, but neither of us *know* she's there, do we, Tom?'

Lepski made a noise like a circular saw hitting a knot of wood.

'So what? We get a warrant and raid the place. We find Mrs Jamison! Or we don't . . . so what?'

'Tom, you are a good cop,' Terrell said, 'but you don't know a thing about the politics of this city. There are three judges here who could sign a warrant, but they won't for the simple fact they are Loveheart's weekly clients. The Mayor is also her client. We can not, repeat can not, raid Loveheart's whore-house. I'm not saying you are wrong, but if Mrs Jamison isn't there you and I will be retired. Make no mistake about that. Lucy has too much clout going for her. So forget it! We wait until the ransom is paid and Mrs Jamison is safe, then we'll grab Lucan, this tough and the Viet, but we stay still until then.'

With a grunt of disgust, Lepski got to his feet and stamped out of Terrell's office.

Having had a three-pill sleep, Lucan came awake, and his thoughts immediately turned to the lush girl next door. He shaved, showered and put on swim-shorts. He decided he would invite her to have a swim, then take her to lunch, then soften her up with sweet talk, and by the evening she should be a push-over.

Flexing his muscles, he left his cabin and rapped on Beryl's cabin door. There was a pause, then the door opened and, to Lucan's startled dismay, he found himself confronted by a tall, powerfully built man who gave him a wide, friendly smile.

'I'm Jack Shaddock,' Howard Jackson said, and reaching out, grabbed Lucan's hand in a vice-like grip and shook it. I guess you're Julian Lucan.' He released Lucan's half paralysed hand. 'My little wife tells me you were good enough to feed her last night. Thanks a million. My wife likes to eat.' Jackson gave a booming laugh. 'I've just arrived. Some place, huh?'

All Lucan's erotic thoughts about getting Beryl into his bed faded. He forced a smile.

'Just being neighbourly. I thought as she was on her own, she'd like a swim. Well, that's okay. I guess I'll take off.'

'Yeah,' Jackson said. 'We won't be staying long. I've a big deal on.' The two men stared at each other. Jackson's smile was less friendly. 'See you around,' he went on, and closed the door.

As Lucan, feeling utterly frustrated, walked down to the sea, he experienced an odd uneasiness. He shrugged this off, telling himself it was due to his frustration. As he waded into the sea, he tried to cheer himself up by thinking there were still lots of women around.

It wasn't until he was stretched out under the shade of a palm tree that this odd feeling of uneasiness returned. Then suddenly a cold shiver ran down his back.

When he had been confronted by this man who called himself Jack Shaddock, something at the back of his mind told Lucan he had seen this man before.

Lucan had a photographic memory for faces: this was part of his way of life. As he lay on the sand, a picture came into his mind of a big, powerfully built man striding down a street in Miami. Lucan had been talking to a black man who was trying to persuade him to help him handle his string of hustlers.

The black man nudged Lucan.

'See that fink?' he had said in a whisper. 'Remember

him. That's Howard Jackson, the FBI agent in this town. You run up against him, and you run into trouble.'

That had been three years ago

Lucan sat up, cold sweat oozing out of him.

Yes!

Jack Shaddock was Howard Jackson, an FBI agent!

His mind in utter panic, Lucan stared at the sea. It took him several minutes to get his panic under control. Beryl must be an FBI plant! This could only mean that the FBI suspected that he had something to do with the kidnapping, and they were watching him!

He got unsteadily to his feet and walked back to his cabin.

With the cabin door shut, Lucan went to the liquor-cabinet and poured himself a triple Scotch. Then he sat down. He drank and moaned to himself.

The FBI!

He moaned again. How could he have been so crazy as to have got himself involved with a man like Kling?

Greed, of course!

He had been mesmerized by the thought of owning five hundred thousand dollars.

What was a sum like that compared to his freedom? He knew if there was a slip-up, and with the FBI watching him, he could go behind bars for at least ten years!

He must leave at once! He would return to New York! He would find another old, fat woman who would keep him in luxury. Yes! He must leave at once!

Finishing his drink, he jumped to his feet and rushed into the bedroom. He dressed. Then it took him only half an hour to pack his many clothes in two suitcases.

To hell with five hundred thousand dollars! he kept telling himself.

Out! Out! Out!

For a brief moment, he paused, wondering if he should

alert Kling that they were being watched by FBI agents. No! That could lead to complications. Kling might not let him go. To hell with him!

Lucan went out into the hot sunshine, looked furtively to right and left, then brought his car to the cabin.

Watched by Howard Jackson and Beryl, he threw his suitcases into the car's trunk and drove to the reception desk. There he settled his check, saying he had to return home immediately, then he drove off.

'Are you letting that creep get away?' Beryl asked.

'We can't stop him,' Jackson said. 'So far, we have nothing on him. I guess he must have recognized me and has taken fright. After all, the big catch is the tough and the Vietnamese.'

A few minutes before 20.00, Maurice Felder arrived at the *Baur au Lac* hotel. He was immediately conducted to Sherman Jamison's suite where he found Jamison pacing restlessly up and down the big living-room. He saw a table was laid for dinner, and this pleased Felder who liked good food.

'Ah, there you are, Felder,' Jamison said, shaking hands. 'No doubt you have news for me. Dinner will be served at once, then we can talk.'

Even as he was speaking, there came a tap on the door, and two waiters pushed a trolley into the room.

'A simple meal,' Jamison said. 'Smoked salmon, *carrée d'agneau* and cheese. I understand they have a bottle of Margaux '61 which should be drinkable.'

The two men sat at the table. While eating the thick slices of smoked salmon, Felder, aware that Jamison didn't want to talk about immediate business as the waiters remained in the room, talked about Zurich, the weather, the currency situation and the strengthening of the dollar. He was an expert at harmless small talk.

Jamison, who hadn't eaten since he had flown from Paradise City, ate well. He grunted, nodded, but made no effort to contribute to Felder's gentle flow of waffle.

Finally the meal ended. The waiters removed the dishes. It was then that Jamison came alive. He stared at Felder.

'Now . . . what have you to tell me?'

'I believe, Mr Jamison, with your approval, I have solved your problem,' Felder said, relaxing back in an armchair and fingering the balloon glass of cognac the waiter had poured before leaving. 'I don't think I need to tell you that an American citizen, residing in the States, is not allowed to have un *undeclared* bank account in Switzerland. Further, although the Swiss banks will accept payments, they will not accept money that can be proved comes from criminal sources. This man Kling is a resident of the States and an American citizen. For the past five or six years, he has been using the Bovay Bank to pay in sums of money. Henri Bovay appears to be in debt to this man . . . some important favour, but we need not go into that. He has allowed Kling to pay in money without question of its origin. I have talked to Paul Bovay. He understands the problem. He is more than willing to co-operate.' Felder paused to sip his excellent cognac. 'I suggest, Mr Jamison, you pay into Kling's account the five-million-dollar ransom demand. Bovay will notify Kling that the money has been placed to his credit.'

'How will he do that?' Jamison asked.

'Naturally, Kling wouldn't want an official receipt. Some letters with Swiss stamps are often examined by the American authorities. So it has been agreed between Henri Bovay and Kling that when money has been received into his account, he will receive a tourist postcard. In this case, he will get a postcard saying "Five of your friends are hoping to see you soon" and signed with Bovay's initials. That will tell Kling the five million has been paid into his account.'

Jamison nodded.

'Then . . . ?'

'Bovay will then alert the Zurich police that he has received ransom money and the kidnapper will claim it. Kling will have to come to the bank to claim the money and he will be arrested.' Felder paused, then went on, 'By the time it takes Kling to fly to Zurich, he will have released Mrs Jamison, convinced he has the money, and she will be safe.'

'No,' Jamison thought, his face expressionless, 'she will be dead, and I will be free to marry Tarnia.'

'You are sure this postcard will convince Kling the money has been paid?'

'Bovay tells me so,' Felder said. 'Yes, I think there is no doubt about that.'

'Then I see no reason why my wife shouldn't be released.' Jamison sat back, thinking. Yes! he told himself, as soon as Kling got the postcard he would murder Shannon. He now wanted to be rid of Felder so he could take a long, earnest look at this dangerous and complicated situation.

'You have done extremely well, Felder,' he said, and got to his feet. 'Thank you. I take it the Organization will advance the five million quickly?'

'No problem, Mr Jamison. We have plenty of liquid assets.' Felder felt he was being dismissed. He hurriedly swallowed the last of the cognac and got to his feet.

'I suppose it will take a few days for the postcard to reach Kling?' Jamison asked.

'Oh no. It will be sent express. I would say not more than two days.'

'Have it addressed to Kling at the Star Motel, Paradise City. Kling is staying there. Go ahead, Felder, don't let us waste any time.'

The two men shook hands and Jamison ushered Felder from his suite.

He then sat down, lit a cigar and considered the situation.

Before leaving Zurich he had hit on what seemed to him to be a safe solution to avoid paying Kling.

Kling's plan for the police to find Shannon's dead body in the trunk of a stolen car, plus two hundred thousand dollars, should convince the police that the kidnapper, who must be an amateur, had panicked, killed Shannon and bolted, leaving the ransom.

If the police accepted that, then no suspicion could fall on either Kling or himself.

Once Kling was convinced that he (Jamison) had carried out his side of the bargain, and Kling had received the postcard from his Swiss bank, he, being the professional that he was, would carry out his part of the bargain.

But by murdering Shannon Kling would deliver himself into Jamison's hands.

When Kling discovered he had been gypped of five million dollars, he would not dare carry out his threat to go to the District Attorney and report he had been hired by Jamison to kidnap Shannon and had done so, with no intention of harming her. Those tapes he had of his conversation with Jamison would no longer be incriminating *unless Kling was prepared to face trial for murder.* Jamison was sure that Kling, who had apparently no police record, would not risk being tried for murder. Kidnapping, yes, but murder, no! Even with the influence of the Mafia behind him, Kling would most certainly have to serve a lengthy prison sentence.

Jamison nodded, satisfied with his thinking.

He would now have to wait until the postcard arrived. Then he would see Kling again. Once he was sure Kling had murdered Shannon, he would tell Kling not to go to his Swiss bank to collect his money as the Swiss police would be waiting to arrest him. Kling would have to accept the fact that Jamison had outwitted him, and would fade out of the picture.

Jamison frowned.

But would Kling fade out of the picture?

Jamison reminded himself he was dealing with a ruthless, professional killer. When he told Kling that he wasn't getting the money, he might fly into a rage, produce his gun and kill him.

Jamison thought about this. There was this unpleasant possibility. He must take precautions. He decided he would write out the whole account of his meeting with Lucan, his meeting with Kling, how Shannon's murder had been arranged. He would include every detail. There would be no question of calling in a stenographer. He would have to do this himself.

Well, he told himself, he had all night. When the document was completed, he would send it to his attorney: *To be opened in the event of my death*. He would borrow a photocopy machine from the hotel and have a copy for Felder, and certainly a copy for Kling. That would mean he would not have to see Kling again.

He moved to the desk, sat down, found paper and in his small, neat handwriting began to write.

Ng Vee returned to the Star Motel a little after 13.00. He found Kling still in bed, still nursing his hangover, and in a surly mood.

'Where the hell have you been?' Kling snarled.

'Excuse me, sir,' Ng said. 'I gave the lady lunch. Can I get you something?'

Kling glared at him.

'She's got food there, hasn't she? What's the matter with you? She'll be dead in a few days, so what the hell?'

Ng flinched.

'Can I get you something, sir?'

'No. Leave me alone!'

Ng went into the kitchen and closed the door.

168

She'll be dead in a few days!

Tonight he would go to Jamison's villa and kill him. That was the solution. That was the only solution!

Sitting on the edge of the kitchen table, Ng thought back on the three hours he had spent with Shannon Jamison.

Wonderful, marvellous hours!

While he had been preparing lunch for her, she had come into the little kitchen and had talked, while she watched him cook. Little by little, she encouraged him to talk about himself. Her quiet, calm voice was a delight to him.

He told her about his life in Saigon, about his mother, and how his master had rescued him from starvation.

Shannon was careful not to inquire about this man who Ng called his master. She was now certain that this odd youth was desperately in love with her. She felt relief and conidence, sure she could rely on him.

She had insisted that he should share the meal with her, and as they sat opposite each other she had told him about her love for music, a little about her religious faith, and as the meal was finishing she told him she was unable to have a child and how disappointed her husband was.

Ng listened, enraptured that she should take him so much into her confidence. He nearly told her that her husband was planning her murder, but he refrained. This wasn't the time. First, he had to get rid of Jamison, then he would set her free.

She had praised his cooking and when he had cleared the dishes, asking her to leave them, as he would return the following day, she touched his hand.

'Thank you, Kim. You have been very kind to me.'

That night, after Kling had shaken off his hangover and had gone down to the Casino, Ng walked the two miles to Jamison's villa.

Not knowing that Jamison was in Zurich, Ng spent four frustrating hours, hidden in Jamison's garden, waiting and watching.

There were no lights showing in the lower rooms. He saw Smyth leave the villa and walk over to Conklin's garage apartment.

Finally, he decided that Jamison wasn't going to appear. He didn't want his master to return and find him absent.

Well, tomorrow night, he thought, as he began the long hot walk back to the motel, he would try again.

This man must be killed!

The following morning, Kling was in a better mood. After demolishing eggs and waffles, he said to Ng, 'Let's go have a swim, kid.'

All Ng's thoughts were now directed to Shannon.

'I thought, sir, I would see the lady and prepare her lunch,' he said, not looking at Kling.

Kling regarded him, suddenly suspicious.

'What goes on, kid?' he demanded. 'You're not falling for that woman, are you?'

Ng felt his mouth turn dry.

'Oh, no, sir,' he said, clearing the table. 'I just thought . . .'

'You prepare *my* lunch,' Kling growled. 'Never mind about her. She hasn't long to live, and there's food there. Come on. Let's swim.'

She hasn't long to live!

Ng nearly cried out. Controlling himself, he carried the dishes into the kitchen, then went to his room and put on swim-shorts.

The two men, watched by Howard Jackson from his cabin window, went down to the sea.

As Ng swam he told himself he must be very careful. On no account must his master know of his feelings for Shannon. So, when after lunch, Kling said he wanted to be driven to Key West to look at the scene, Ng, with sinking heart, kept his face expressionless. As he drove, he kept thinking of Shannon, wondering what she was doing, and wondering and hoping she wouldn't be disappointed that he hadn't visited her.

Kling, apparently enjoying himself, went around Key West, visited the usual tourists' haunts while Ng went with him.

They didn't return to the Star Motel until 19.00.

'Quite an outing, kid,' Kling said. 'Well, me for a shower and I'll go to the Casino. How about you? Want to come along?'

'Thank you, sir, but I will stay here.' Ng thought he must return to Jamison's villa in the hope the man he planned to kill would be there.

'Please yourself, kid,' Kling said, and went into his bedroom.

Half an hour later, Kling, showered, shaved and wearing a lightweight suit, came into the living-room where Ng was polishing the dining-table.

'I'm off,' Kling said. 'Don't wait up for me. I'll be late.'

'Yes, sir.'

Kling started to move to the door, then paused.

With his evil grin, he said, 'Give me the key of the Whipping room, kid. I think I'd better keep it,' and he held out his hand.

Ng felt as if a fist of iron had hit him under his heart. Somehow, he managed to keep his face expressionless.

'But, sir . . .' he began, but Kling cut him short.

With a snarl in his voice, he barked, 'Give it to me!'

Slowly Ng took the precious key from his pocket and Kling snatched it from him.

'See you, kid,' he said with his evil grin and, dropping the key into his pocket, he left the cabin.

For a long moment of despair Ng stood motionless. He

had first planned to visit Shannon before going to Jamison's villa. Now Kling had taken the key, this visit would be impossible. But why had Kling demanded the key?

Ng groaned to himself. His master must have guessed he was in love with this lovely woman!

The only solution was to kill Jamison!

Leaving the cabin, he walked the two hot miles to Jamison's villa, arriving in the dark.

He wasn't to know that Jamison was in New York, having flown back from Zurich, and didn't plan to return to Paradise City until the following day so Ng had another weary, frustrated wait for more than four hours without seeing Jamison.

The following morning, as Ng, who had spent a sleepless night, was preparing Kling's breakfast, he hard a rap on the cabin door. He found one of the bus-boys who thrust a card at him.

'For Mr Kling,' the boy said. 'Express.'

When the boy left, Ng stared at the card. He saw it had a Swiss stamp and a Zurich postmark.

Scrawled on the card was the message:

Five of your best friends are waiting to see you here.

Ng felt a chill run through him. What did this mean? Could it mean . . . ? He shivered, then he heard Kling come out of his bedroom.

'Sir,' he said. 'Something for you.'

Kling, who had spent a good evening on the beach with a plump redhead, was in a good mood. He took the card, read the message, then released a soft yell of triumph that made Ng stiffen.

'Kid! We're home!' Kling said, and gave Ng a slight punch on his chest. 'I've got the money! Kid! Can you believe it? I'm worth five million dollars! *Five million dollars!* You hear me?'

'Yes, sir.' Ng felt so bad he wanted to throw up. 'I'll get your breakfast,' and he went into the kitchen.

So his plan to save Shannon by killing Jamison was no more. Trembling, he served the two eggs and grilled ham on a plate and put it before Kling who was seated at the table, humming and rubbing his hands.

'Let's talk, kid,' Kling said. 'Sit down. Aren't you eating anything?'

'No, sir.' His legs weak, Ng sat down at the table.

'You're a character, kid, but I like you,' Kling said as he began to eat. 'Remember when we first met? You dirty and starving? They've been good days since then together, haven't they?'

Ng gulped.

'Yes, sir.'

'You and I are going far, kid,' Kling said. 'I've got five million beautiful dollars! I'll hire a yacht, and we'll go together around the world. You'll like that, won't you?'

Ng leaned forward and poured coffee into Kling's cup.

'Kid, you have a job to do,' Kling went on. 'This evening, I want you to knock off a car with a big trunk. A Caddy would be fine.' He munched the ham. 'This is good, kid. You're a great cook.'

Ng found he couldn't speak. He sat motionless, horror in his heart.

'You know, kid, I get the idea you've gone soft on this woman,' Kling went on, cutting into the second egg. 'Okay. It happens. So, all you have to do is to knock off a big car, and I'll do the rest.'

'You are not going to kill her, sir?' Ng asked, his voice scarcely above a whisper.

Kling pushed aside his finished meal and began to butter toast.

'Kid, you're getting your lines crossed. You haven't been paying attention to what I've already told you, so I'll tell you

173

again. I am a professional killer. I make a contract with some guy to knock off some guy or some woman. When I get paid, I do the job. So, okay, Jamison has paid me five million bucks. It is in my Swiss bank right now, so I carry out the contract. All I'm asking you to do is to knock off a car. I'll do the rest. Got it?'

Watching Kling spread marmalade on his toast, Ng shivered.

No! This must not happen! A thought flashed through his mind. By casually getting up to begin to clear the table, he could kill Kling, but that was an impossible thought after what Kling had done for him and for his mother. There must be some other way to save this lovely woman.

His face expressionless, he said, 'I understand, sir. When do you want the car?'

'Tonight, around ten o'clock. I want you to put the car in Loveheart's garage and leave the ignition key in the lock. That's all. You leave the rest to me.' Kling munched his toast. 'Okay?'

'Yes, sir.' Ng got to his feet and cleared the table and went into the kitchen.

The telephone bell rang. Frowning, Kling picked up the receiver.

'Kling?'

Kling recognized Jamison's barking voice.

'Sure.'

'The money is now in your bank,' Jamison said. 'You will now carry out our agreement?'

'No problem.'

'When?'

'Tonight. How about the money to be left?'

'I've arranged that. It will be in a briefcase at the American Express in the name of Hugh Pilby. They have been given instructions to give the briefcase to you without question.'

'That's fine. Around eleven tonight, I'll call you and give

you the number of the car. It'll be parked in the Casino parking lot. Then it's all yours.'

'Right. I am relying on you,' and Jamison hung up.

Getting to his feet, Kling went into the kitchen.

'It's all set, kid,' he said. 'When you knock off this car, park it by the elevator in Loveheart's garage and leave the trunk lid open so I can spot it. As soon as the job's done, we get out fast.'

Ng shuddered.

'Yes, sir.'

'Okay. I've a little business to fix down town. You pack our stuff and be ready to leave late tonight. I'll see you sometime this afternoon.'

'Yes, sir.'

Kling suddenly frowned.

'Hey! I haven't seen that creep Lucan for a couple of days. Have you?'

'No, sir.'

Kling paused for a long moment, thinking, then going to the telephone, he called the reception desk and asked to be connected to Lucan's cabin.

'Mr Lucan checked out two days ago,' the girl told him. 'He left no forwarding address.'

Kling replaced the receiver and stared thoughtfully out of the window.

Why? he wondered. What had caused Lucan to panic? Or maybe he hadn't panicked, but had dropped out of sight until the Jamison woman had been fixed. That would be typical of a spineless creep like Lucan. Too bad for him! When the job was done, he would come whining for his money. By that time, Kling and Ng would be in Zurich, and Lucan would never see the money.

Leaving the cabin, Kling drove down to the American Express offices.

* * *

175

Ng, tormented, spent the day in the cabin. He kept thinking of Shannon. He thought of going to the Whipping room and forcing the lock, then getting her out, but he remembered the lock. It was one of those efficient locks such that when you turned the key, a steel bar shifted into slots, and the only way to get into the room would be to batter down the door with an axe. That could only be done with a great deal of noise. No! That wasn't the solution! But he was determined to rescue Shannon.

As he began packing Kling's clothes, he thought of him. He owed him so much! But the thought of Kling going into that room and murdering Shannon was more than he could bear. He would have to be disloyal! He knew he couldn't persuade Kling not to do this dreadful thing, so he had to stop him!

He spent the rest of the afternoon, praying, asking for guidance. He was still praying when he heard Kling come into the cabin.

Hurriedly getting off his knees, he went into the living-room.

'All fixed, kid,' Kling said, putting a briefcase on the table. 'Packing done?'

'Yes, sir.'

'Fine. Here's the programme. We leave here around ten o'clock. I've checked us out. I've got flight tickets on the one A.M. to New York. We'll spend the night there, and then fly on to Zurich. We can get something to eat on the plane. I'm going for a last swim. Coming?'

'No, thank you, sir,' Ng said. 'I haven't quite finished my own packing.'

'Okay,' and, going into his bedroom, Kling stripped off and put on a pair of swim-shorts that Ng had left out.

That kid thinks of everything, Kling thought. Then taking a towel, he walked down to the sea.

Three hours later it was dark.

'I guess we'll move,' Kling said. He had been watching TV while Ng had remained in the kitchen.

Ng came into the living-room.

'We'll drive down to a car park. I'll leave you there,' Kling said, getting to his feet. 'You may have a little trouble knocking off the right car. There's a big car park near Loveheart's joint. When I've dropped you, I'll go to the car park and wait. I'll give you half an hour, then I'll leave our car in the park, and walk the rest of the way. You know what to do. Don't forget to leave the lid of the trunk half open and park close to the elevator, then you return to our car and wait for me.'

Ng drew in a shuddering breath.

'Yes, sir.'

'Put our cases in our car now, kid,' Kling said, 'and we'll go.'

He waited until Ng, carrying the suitcases, had gone out into the darkness, then he took from his pocket a short length of electric cable. At the ends of the cable were small wood handles: the favourite killing weapon used by the Mafia. He tested the handles, then, satisfied, he returned the garotte to his pocket.

Leaving the lights on in the living-room, he went out to join Ng who was already sitting in the car.

It so happened that Howard Jackson and Beryl were seated at the table, eating sandwiches. They didn't see Ng place the bags in the car's trunk, but they heard the car start up.

Jackson kicked back his chair and went to the window in time to see the red rear lights of Kling's car shoot away down the sandy road. He stepped out into the hot, humid night, moved to where he could see Kling's cabin. He saw the sitting-room window, curtains drawn, was showing lights.

He returned to where Beryl was finishing her sandwich.

'He's gone out for the evening, leaving the Viet,' he said, and sitting down, picked up another sandwich.

Detective 1st Grade Tom Lepski sat in his car outside the Casino in the dreary hope there would be some action.

The time was 22.15.

Lepski had had an unexpectedly good chicken-on-the-spit dinner that, more by luck than judgement, Carroll had cooked to perfection. The apple pie wasn't all it should be, but after cutting away most of the burnt crust Lepski had enjoyed it.

As he sat in his seat, relaxed, he thought of Shannon Jamison's kidnapping. The biggest sensation ever in Paradise City, and yet Chief of Police Terrell refused to make a move.

Lepski was certain that Shannon Jamison was holed up in Lucy Loveheart's flesh emporium, and yet, because all the top-shots of the city patronized the place, the police were prohibited to raid it!

As soon as the ransom is paid, then we move in fast.

Lepski snorted. When the hell was the ransom going to be paid? Jamison had said he would alert Terrell once he had his wife back, then, possibly, it would be too late to catch the kidnappers.

Bored with staring bleakly at the Casino entrance, watching the rich get out of their cars and enter, eager to lose their money, Lepski decided to drive down to the harbour where there just might be some action.

He started his car and drove slowly through the dense traffic down to where the rich moored their luxury yachts.

He parked in the shadows, sat back, lit a cigarette and surveyed the scene. At this time, there was a lot of activity: tourists gaping at the yachts and motor cruisers, parties going on deck with men in tuxedos and women flashing

178

their diamonds, eating, drinking and talking at the top of their voices.

He switched on his two-way radio.

'Charlie? Tom. I'm down by the harbour. Any action?'

'Not your kind, Tom,' Tanner replied. 'We've just had an alert that a car belonging to Mr van Roberts was stolen twenty minutes ago.'

'Cars!' Lepski moaned. 'Some goddamn kid! Okay, let's have it. I'll watch for it.'

'Dark red Caddy. No. PC5544.'

'Okay.' Lepski scribbled the number down on a pad. 'I'll watch out.'

'All partols have been alerted. Mr van Roberts is VIP and he's hopping mad.'

'Yeah, who isn't VIP except you and me?' Lepski snorted and switched off.

He went back to staring at the crowds on the waterfront.

For the past twenty minutes, Kling had been sitting in his car in the parking lot near Lucy Loveheart's residence, smoking and waiting. His eyes constantly went to his watch.

While he waited, he thought of what he would do with five million dollars. He grinned to himself. For the first time in his dangerous life, he would be worth real money. He wondered how the kid was getting on. He would get a car and deliver it according to Kling's instructions. Kling had no doubt about that. Not once had the kid taken a wrong step. It was odd that he seemed to have turned a bit soft about the woman, but that didn't matter. The kid was young. When they reached Zurich and had collected the money, Kling would see if he could fix the kid up with some chick. That's what the kid needed: to screw and be screwed. It would make all the difference to the kid's outlook.

Kling again looked at his watch. Time to go! He slid out of his car. He paused to check that he had the key to the

Whipping room, then he put his hand inside his other pocket and fingered the garotte. It would be quick, and no mess, he thought, as he set off along the sidewalk, keeping in the shadows.

Checking that no one was observing him, he walked quickly down the ramp to the underground garage that was lit by one overhead lamp.

Parked a few yards from the elevator was a glittering red Cadillac with the lid of the trunk half open.

Kling nodded to himself. Nice work, kid, he thought. Very nice work.

He pressed the down button of the elevator and when the cage arrived, he stepped in and thumbed the top floor button.

When the elevator came to a stop, Kling took out the garotte. He stepped into the passage and looked up and down the dimly lit corridor, listened, then moved over to the door of the Whipping room.

Silently he inserted the key and turned it gently, then eased open the door.

The sound of a Mozart concerto from the radio greeted him. He slid forward, leaving the door ajar, the garotte dangling in his fingers.

He saw her, sitting with her back to him, intent on the music, and his evil smile lit up.

Too easy! he thought, and moved like a phantom towards her. The garotte now a loop, ready to drop over her head.

Then steel-like fingers closed around the back of his neck. He felt a rush of blood to his head. He made an effort to claw away the fingers, then blackness descended, and he fell forward with a thump on the carpet.

With a scream, Shannon sprang to her feet and turned. She saw the Vietnamese youth staring down at a man who lay face down.

She began to back away, suppressing another scream.

'Quick, ma'am!' Ng gasped. 'I am getting you out of here! Please come with me! We have only a few minutes before he recovers. Quick!'

Shannon, seeing the tragic expression on Ng's face, immediately realizing he had come to rescue her, went to him.

Taking her by the wrist, he hurried her to the elevator. In the garage, he got her into the stolen Cadillac, slid under the steering-wheel and started the engine. He swept around and drove fast up the ramp onto the street.

'Don't say anything, ma'am,' he said. 'Listen, please. This is a stolen car. By now they will be looking for it. I haven't much time.'

'Oh, Kim!' Shannon gasped. 'I knew you would help me!'

'Yes, ma'am,' Ng said. 'I had to help you.' He swung the car onto a side street that led down to the water-front.

'Was that man your master?' Shannon asked.

'Yes, ma'am.' Ng caught his breath in a sob. 'I have been disloyal. It's something I can't live with. I must tell you, ma'am. Don't go home. Go to a true friend, but don't go home.'

He found himself on the water-front. He had only a vague idea of the geography of the city and, seeing the crowded quay, he slowed the car to a crawl.

'I don't understand what you are saying, Kim.'

'We must talk.' 'Ng saw a parking space and edged the big car between two other cars and cut the engine. He turned to look at her, his face showing suffering and tear marks. 'Ma'am, please believe me. It was your husband who wanted to get rid of you. He hired my master to murder you. He paid five million dollars.'

'Oh, no!' Shannon gasped.

'Please, believe me,' Ng said and gripped her wrist. 'You must keep away from him! He wants a child! Go to some friend who you can trust, but don't go home. You understand?'

Shannon felt an icy chill run through her. Thinking of the last time she had talked to her husband, seeing his ruthless face, she realized this wasn't fantasy.

Somewhere safe? Meg Clayton!

While they were talking, Lepski shifted his eyes to a newly parked car, then stiffened.

Red Caddy. No. PC 5544.

Goddamn it! he thought. Here's the stolen car! He leaned forward and peered through his windshield. He saw there was a man and a woman, sitting side by side in the front seat.

Action at last!

He reached for his two-way radio.

'Charlie! That Caddy is parked on quay eight. Man and woman in it. Block all exits to the quay. I'm investigating.'

'Will do,' Tanner said and switched off.

Lepski eased his gun in its holster, then, leaving his jacket hanging open, he slid out of his car and threaded his way through the tourists to the Cadillac. He arrived at the driver's open window and immediately recognized Ng. His gun jumped into his hand.

'Police,' he growled in his cop voice. 'Come on out, both of you, and come carefully.'

Ng looked at Shannon.

'Ma'am, please remember what I said. Don't go home,' and, opening the car door, he got out.

'You too!' Lepski snapped.

Shannon got out of the car and, moving swiftly, came around to join Ng.

There came the sound of police sirens as patrol cars converged on the quay.

Moving between Ng and Lepski, Shannon said quietly, 'I am Mrs Sherman Jamison. I have been kidnapped. This young man has rescued me.'

Lepski gaped at her.

'You're Mrs Jamison?'

'Yes.'

He stared at her, and then recognized her. He had often seen photographs of her in the press.

Two police cars, their blue lamps flashing, came from either end of the quay and men spilled out.

Lepski suddenly realized the Vietnamese was no longer there. With a movement as quick as a lizard, Ng had jumped towards the harbour wall, and with another jump, as Lepski raised his gun, there was a splash of water.

Ng swam under water until he was clear of the yachts, then he surfaced and trod water, looking for the last time at Shannon who was standing motionless, her hands covering her face.

God bless you, ma'am, he thought, then let himself sink into the oily water. The debris from the yachts closed over him.

Kling recovered consciousness to find himself lying on the plush carpet of the Whipping room. His brain immediately became alive. Staggering to his feet, he looked around, but he knew Shannon Jamison had gone and the kid had gone with her. He stood still for some moments until he felt himself again, then, snarling, he searched the apartment, not expecting to find the two there, but he looked.

Again he paused to think. So the little bastard, after serving him like a slave with his 'No problem, sir' had double-crossed him because he had fallen for a woman!

Snatching up the garotte from the floor, Kling left the Whipping room, shutting the door, but leaving the key in the lock.

He rode down in the elevator to the garage and saw the stolen Cadillac had gone. Ng wouldn't get far. The cops would spot the car, and he'd go away in the slammer for at least ten years. Serve the little bastard right!

Kling's one thought now was to get out. To hell with Jamison! He told himself that he had to get to Zurich. He had his flight reservations, his clothes and two hundred thousand dollars from Jamison in his car.

He ran up the ramp of the garage and in a few minutes he was driving fast to the Miami airport.

It wasn't until he had checked in and boarded the New York flight, that he settled himself in his first-class seat and relaxed.

Zurich, here I come! he thought and grinned. He would collect the five million dollars and drop out of sight. As the plane took off, he began to hum softly. Five million dollars! he was thinking, but he wasn't to know that three Swiss detectives were sitting in the entrance hall of the Bovay Bank waiting to arrest him.

Jamison sat at his desk. He kept looking at his watch. The time was 23.15. Why no word from Kling? Had something gone wrong? He felt confident, now that Kling had proof the money was in his bank, he would murder Shannon. Why this exasperating wait? He felt his heart beating unevenly and he forced himself to remain patient.

There came a tap on the door, and he barked, 'Come in!' Smyth came in and placed a letter before him.

'An express, sir, just come in.'

Jamison looked at the letter and saw the Italian stamps. At last! A letter from Tarnia.

'Thank you, Smyth. Get me sandwiches. I will be up late.'

'Certainly, sir.' Smyth bowed and left the room. He went into the pantry and prepared two chicken and ham sandwiches and two smoked-salmon sandwiches. He added a few leaves of fresh lettuce, then carried the plate to Jamison's study.

He stood in the open doorway, staring.

Jamison, still in his chair, was lying face down across the desk.

'Sir!' Smyth exclaimed. 'Is something wrong?'

Jamison didn't move.

Putting down the silver plate, Smyth went to him. He saw in a moment that Jamison was dead, and he also saw, clutched in Jamison's fingers, a letter.

Shocked, Smyth took the letter from the dead man's hand. He hesitated for a long moment, then read the letter.

Rome.

Dear Sherry,

I do hope you will be understanding. I have decided I don't want to get married either to you nor to any other man. Guiseppi has offered me a partnership in his wonderful, enormously successful fashion house. The firm will be known as Guiseppi & Lawrence. I am sure you will realize what this must mean to me.

Sherry, I am sorry, but I do hope you will find someone else who will be a mother to your children.

Forgive me?

Tarnia.

>>> If you've enjoyed this book and would like to discover more great vintage crime and thriller titles, as well as the most exciting crime and thriller authors writing today, visit: >>>

The Murder Room
Where Criminal Minds Meet

themurderroom.com